S0-COO-447

FULL SAIL FOR TRIPOLI

F
Gra

Full Sail for Tripoli

BY WILLIAM R. GRAYDON

6988

GOLDEN GATE JUNIOR BOOKS
SAN CARLOS, CALIFORNIA

PROPERTY OF
CURTIS BAPTIST CHURCH LIBRARY
AUGUSTA, GEORGIA

Full sail for Tripoli,
JF Gra 14780
Graydon, William R.
Curtis Baptist Elem. School

Copyright © 1968 by William R. Graydon
All rights reserved
Library of Congress catalog card number 68-25857
Lithographed in the United States of America
by Anderson, Ritchie & Simon, Los Angeles

The author wishes to express special thanks to Mrs. Louise Tudor for manuscript preparation and editing, and to "old salts" Scotty Stewart and George Tapper for their solid contributions to a seaworthy craft.

FULL SAIL FOR TRIPOLI

CHAPTER I

ANDY FOLGER felt the deck coming up to meet him as the grapeshot smashed into the hull. Slammed to the deck as the blast from the enemy cannon roared in his ears, he dug his fingernails desperately into the wooden planking in an effort to make himself as small a target as possible. Already smoke was pouring back from the *Enterprise's* own guns as he steeled himself to return to his post at the port battery.

Gunner Ransom shot him an anxious glance as the slender youth pulled himself slowly to his feet. "Hurt, lad?"

Andy felt the slight cut on his cheek made by a flying splinter, shook his head dazedly, and made ready to help reload the gun. Acrid smoke from the batteries of both ships, blazing away at close range, swirled over him, making it difficult to see much of anything. Through a break in the man-made haze, he could distinguish several gaping holes in the mainsails and topgallant and a few smaller ones in the flag that fluttered above them. Even now, in the fury of action, it made his heart beat more rapidly to see Old Glory, with its fifteen stripes and stars, standing out before the breeze.

Then, as suddenly as it had begun, the battle was over. There was a brief, disbelieving interval of silence, followed almost immediately by a throaty roar that reechoed throughout the ship as the tars and marines gave full voice to their enthusiasm.

It was a moment of grand confusion. Cheering men thumped each other on the back and two seamen hugged each other as they danced an impromptu jig, adding their voices to the general din. Andy straightened up cautiously, peered over the bulwark, and finally got his first close-up look at the Tripolitan man-o-war.

The *Enterprise* had taken a beating all right, but the enemy cruiser had fared far worse. Her sails were mere shrouds, ripped and torn, with the shreds flapping in the breeze and a jagged break showing where her foremast had been snapped by a cannon ball. Judging from the running account Gunner Ransom had given his crew as he bobbed up and down in excitement, Andy believed their cannister shot must have taken a heavy toll on the cruiser's deck as the two ships fought it out at close quarters. Now, looking beyond the beaten ship, he was startled to notice that the azure-blue waters of the Mediterranean still sparkled in the brilliant afternoon sunshine, unmindful of the violent sea battle that had just been fought.

Andy's heart skipped a beat as the *Enterprise* grappled to her conquered victim and the United States Marines swarmed over her. Moments later, he watched nervously as the unkempt Tripolitan prisoners were herded on board — bloody, sweaty, and dirty. Some of the more seriously wounded were being carried by their shipmates. Others glared at their captors ferociously, looking like trapped animals that expected to be executed on the spot.

The cabin boy knew they would receive fair treatment from Captain Decatur but, evidently, the corsairs did not. Either way, the closely guarded prisoners were not the sort of men he would like to meet at the end of a saber or pike on a dark night. He was certain, too, that, had the situation been reversed, the Americans would have been assured of no such treatment from the Pasha of Tripoli. He had heard about the Pasha's way with prisoners and, even now, his palms grew sweaty at the thought. Deep inside, Andy could not shake the desperate notion that if the enemy had boarded the *Enterprise,* he would have abandoned his post and run like a rabbit, seeking out the deepest, darkest cranny of the ship in which to hide. Grimly, he hoped none of the others could read his mind. Unconsciously, he shrank back as the captured enemy sailors were led to the after-hold.

The mess boy stole a quick glance at the quarterdeck where Captain Stephen Decatur stood viewing the spectacle. Wearing dress blues, complete with sword, and eying his prisoners with cool detachment, the young commander of the *Enterprise* looked as though he had just held an inspection of ship's company instead of having defeated a Tripolitan brig in a sharp, bitter three-hour engagement. Only the pistol tucked in his belt and another jammed in his boot indicated that the captain had been ready for any eventuality, including boarding and hand-to-hand combat.

A sharp command from the deck lieutenant cut short Andy's star-gazing. "Here, you two men. You, lad. Get this man below to the surgeon."

Andy turned and for the first time became conscious of the wounded marine lying on the deck a few feet away, a dark splotch of red showing through his shirt. The youth's face blanched and suddenly he felt ill. Bos'n Criter stepped forward to lift the injured man, but the spindly-legged mess boy stood riveted to the spot, memories of his father's accident flooding his mind.

The lieutenant spoke again. "Look lively, lad. Bear a hand."

Andy trembled and the boatswain gave a coarse laugh. "The Mouse is scared stiff at the sight of blood. Here, somebody else give us a hand."

The mess boy flinched at the realization that Criter would never let up on him, never pass up an opportunity to taunt him. He looked down at the wounded marine. Suddenly he tottered. The heat of the battle, the sharp, pungent gun smoke that hovered over the ship, and the sight of the blood made his head spin until the scene became no more than a blur. The last thing he heard before he fainted was the boatswain's grating laughter.

When he came to, the lieutenant and the others were gone. Gunner Ransom was standing by, getting ready to slosh a second bucket of salt water over him. The boy sat up slowly, mopping the water from his face.

He flushed visibly, even his overly large ears turning a dull crimson. "I'm sorry, Guns. I fainted dead away."

"Nothing to that, lad," Ransom replied, resting a kindly hand on the thin shoulders. "Lots of men faint the first time they see blood. Remember that you've had a rough go of it at the guns today. You'll get over it. Now, though, you'd better bend on full sail for the galley. Everybody missed dinner today and I'll wager the officers will want to stow some vittles and guzzle some hot tea after *that* tussle!"

Andy sighed, muttered his mournful thanks, and trudged slowly back toward the galley. As he stepped through the hatch and let himself down the narrow ladder, the banging of pans and kettles roused him from his lethargy. The sight of the little cook succeeded in bringing a half-grin to his face, one which he managed to smother quickly. With sleeves rolled above his pudgy forearms and a long black smudge streaked across his face, Billy Blossom was trying to keep his hat on with one hand and guard his pans against the roll of the ship with the other. The round little man was calling down the wrath of the heavens on the officers, crew, and the pirates as well.

"Scurvy corsairs," he shrilled. "They've kept me from my galley all day. The officers are impatient for their supper and the hands are baying for hot food. How they expect me to turn out anything fit for human consumption is beyond me if they can't hold this ship still for a minute. It'll be a miracle if they get anything but warm salt spray today."

Catching sight of Andy, the little man's round eyes snapped. "So you've decided to favor us with a visit, my lad. I hope you had a pleasant afternoon strolling about the deck and taking in all the sights. Now that you've condescended to join us, maybe you'll get some of this food to the wardroom. Sam's already made one trip and is off on his second. And if I may be so bold as to ask, what kept you from reporting down here right away?"

Andy reddened and his voice was low as he answered sheepishly, "I fainted, Blossom, that's what. By now they're probably laughing about it all over the ship."

Instantly the little man was aquiver with sympathy, his pots and pans forgotten. "You fainted, Andy? During battle?"

"Not quite so bad as all that," replied the boy slowly. "It was after the fight when the first lieutenant ordered me to help a wounded marine to sick bay. I stared at him but my feet just wouldn't move. Then I fainted."

Blossom's sympathetic smile revealed several notable wooden fillings. "Well, it's no wonder, Andy. They keep us up all night standing watch, baking pies and what have you, then make us fight pirates all day without a morsel of food. They expect us to bound about like trained monkeys on a string. Probably you just had a case of sunstroke or something, but maybe it'll show 'em they can't work us like common galley slaves. If I had my way, I'd serve boiled corsair to the hands and jack tar stew to the pirates!"

Andy laughed at this bloodthirsty notion and the pot-bellied little man grinned back, pleased at having snapped the boy's gloomy mood. Blossom's verbal battles with the crew were well known, but no one ever took them seriously and often they served to break tensions built up by long months at sea. Whenever the cook ventured topside he was apt to be the target of their jibes and taunts. But privately the men boasted that Blossom was the best cook in the Navy. Let the hands from another man-o-war make the slightest disparaging remark about Blossom and the crew of the *Enterprise* paid them back quickly and firmly.

Now the door burst open and Sam Plummer came plunging into the galley, an empty tureen in his hand.

"Andy!" shouted the stocky, freckle-faced lad. "I'm ever so glad to set eyes on you again. I'd heard that enemy grape had near scuttled your whole gun crew."

Without waiting for an answer the newcomer grabbed his friend's arm, rattling on exuberantly, "Did we stand the brigands on their heads or didn't we? What a fight! And we bested 'em. We whipped them fair and square!"

"Sam — Andy," exploded Blossom. "You two do your jawing on your own time. You can re-fight the battle back on the fantail when you're off duty. Now you'd better hustle this chow to the hands afore I dent your noggins with this skillet."

Later, chores in the galley completed, the two boys made their way to the stern of the ship where they found two of their close friends, Jaime Rand and Gunner Ransom, discussing the day's events. Andy was relieved greatly to see that neither Bos'n Criter nor any of his cronies were about. Ever since the boy's arrival on board the *Enterprise,* the husky boatswain had persisted in making his life miserable, and Andy was sure that the man would make the most of today's fainting incident.

"The captain's decided to tow our prize into Algiers," Jaime was saying. "You know, the Dey of Algiers spends most of his time balancing on a fence. Half the time he pretends to be neutral, and the other half he's ready to join up with his chums at Tripoli to give piracy a whirl again. Heaven knows, our prizes have been few and far between ever since our squadrons took up the blockade in 1801! That's why I think Captain Decatur will welcome this opportunity to show the Dey that American ships have teeth as well as sail."

Sam and Andy listened respectfully. The blond, curly-headed quartermaster had a way of making sense. Not only did the young Virginian know his navigation thoroughly, but he was a mine of information on other subjects as well. Jaime had been to college, had graduated from William and Mary a few years earlier. Scuttlebutt said he had been offered a commission as an officer and that he had turned it down because he did not want to make the Navy his life's work.

Instead, Jaime had his heart set on becoming a professor of history and was gaining first-hand knowledge of the world while serving his country at the same time. Despite his superior education, the quartermaster never ridiculed the others or flaunted his knowledge pointlessly. When either of the two boys asked him a question, he did his best to answer intelligently. Life on a U.S. man-o-war might be hard but Andy was thankful there were shipmates like Jaime, Gunner Ransom, and Sam Plummer.

Glancing aft at the battered cruiser under tow, Ransom removed the black stub of pipe from his teeth and spat into the ship's wake. "Aye, Jaime, I think the captain does have some such notion in mind. We've been too long in giving the pirates a taste of American metal. Tunisia, Morocco, and Algiers have been getting restless of late. What with our first two squadrons accomplishing next to nothing, the brigands may well have planned to start raiding again. Whipping that ship today won't win the war, but it may serve to put a little fear into those pirates who are thinking of taking up their trade again."

Presently the little group broke up and the tars made their way slowly to their quarters. Andy looked back at the dark hulk of the ship riding astern of them. Even though he could hear the slap of the waves against her hull and see her broken spars outlined against the night sky, it was difficult to believe that the events of the day had been real. It was even more difficult to realize that the *Enterprise* was carrying enemy prisoners to a neutral port.

Climbing wearily into his hammock, he wondered what his friends in New England would think if they saw him now — and how his mother would react to his present surroundings. Lulled by the now-gentle roll of the ship, his thoughts spanned the thousands of miles from the Mediterranean back to the hills of his native Massachusetts. This time of year the leaves would be changing color and the first snow would be coming. It had been months since he had signed into the Navy. This was the longest he had ever been away from home and there were moments when he felt sharp pangs of homesickness — like the day when he passed his fifteenth birthday without so much as a nod or pat on the back from anyone.

Now, unbidden, the events of the day just past flooded over him — the hoarse cry of alarm at sighting the enemy sail on the horizon, Sam and himself tumbling over pots and pans as they scurried to their battle stations, the frenzied pounding in his heart as the long cannon boomed its message across the water. He smelled again the sharp odor of burning powder, heard the splash of steel on wave as the enemy sought their range.

Especially he remembered his own fears, the dryness in his mouth, the trembling at the thought that the enemy might board them, his awkward attempts to keep his shipmates from recognizing that he was a coward. The wounded marine, the lieutenant's unspoken disgust, and Bos'n Criter's undisguised scorn — it was impossible to keep such thoughts from racing through his mind.

It had been his first taste of action, but he knew it would not be his last. And, as he dozed fitfully, Andy found himself wondering about the chain of events that had led him from his snug New England to the blue Mediterranean with its parched, exotic lands and its strange, fierce peoples.

CHAPTER II

As usual, Andy and his father arose before dawn, milked the two cows, fed and watered old Jake, and performed their morning chores. Judging from the rosy glow that tinged the eastern skies with the sun's first shaft of light, the day would be a beauty. Eagerly, the boy sniffed the soft spring breeze. There was something special in the Massachusetts air this morning, something special was about to happen. Yet, seated for breakfast at the pineboard table, Andy's father made usual table conversation, talking crops and the news from the town—in fact, discussing everything but the subject that was uppermost in the boy's mind.

Finally, Andy could stand the suspense no longer. "Father," he broke in, "today's the day, isn't it? You promised — "

The tall, rawboned farmer dug deeply into his steaming stack of wheatcakes, doused them liberally with maple syrup, and broke into a smile.

"Jen." Nate Folger nodded at Andy's mother. "The lad's right. Today we begin work on the cabin. After breakfast, me and Andy will hitch up Jake, take ourselves a ride, and make a start on our new home." He threw one arm around his slim twelve-year-old son. "It'll be mighty handy to have such a fine helper."

Excitement sparkled in his mother's eyes. "Nate, I can scarce believe we're going to have a new cabin. This one does us well, of course, and I'll be sorrowed to leave it, but I think the new location is the prettiest yet."

Andy had to agree with his mother. The site his father had selected for the new home had everything a boy could want. Situated in the Berkshire Highlands at the northern edge of the lovely Connecticut Valley, Andy felt sure it was one of the finest spots in all Massachusetts. Less than a dozen miles from their present cabin, the new location had a good stand of timber, a chipper brook bubbling nearby, and a ground dip that could be flooded easily to make a skating pond when cold weather came. There were hills for sliding, game a-plenty, good fishing close by, and all the blueberries you could eat, just for the picking.

"You're right, Jen," his father was saying. "This home has served us well, but I've learned a good bit since I built this cabin and I promise you that the new one will make your eyes dance. There'll be windows, a sturdy wood floor, and the finest fireplace you've ever seen. You wait and see! We'll be in our new home, snug as bear cubs in a den, long before the first frost."

Later that morning, inspecting the new site with his father, Andy discovered many wonders — for example, the marvelous beaver dam, built of branches and twigs, a short distance upstream. Glancing sidewise at his son, Nate Folger was pleased to see that the boy appeared to be losing some of his natural timidity in the presence of the wonders of nature. He seemed to have forgotten his fear of the forest which ordinarily made him stick close to his father's side. Nate Folger had never known fear in any form and it was painful to see it crop out in his son. To Nate, it was unaccountable. His own ancestors had been rugged frontiersmen, among the first settlers of New England. The boy's mother came of durable pioneer stock also, but there was no denying that at times little Andy was prone to jump at his own shadow. Maybe the fear went back to the day the lad had been surprised by a black bear as he had neared the den where her cubs were sleeping. Or to the time when the Indians had laid waste to a farm nearby and there was talk of a general Indian uprising. Or, maybe fear was simply a part of the lad's nature — and who could explain such a thing as that? Once or twice, Nate had ventured to mention the matter to his wife, but Jen Folger had merely sighed and remarked, "Be patient, Nate. Given time, the lad will outgrow this."

This morning Andy found that watching the beaver dam was great fun, but there was work to be done. Toiling with old Jake, hauling the logs his father felled, made the boy hungry well before noontime. Andy was thinking of the fine lunch his mother had packed for them, and listening to the steady ring of his father's ax and his cheerful whistling when it happened.

The ax made a dull, clunking sound behind him and the whistle gurgled to a choking sigh. Andy spun around sharply and raced back to his father who sat rocking to and fro on the turf, clutching his leg. Blood was spurting from a deep wound above the knee and his father wore a look of pained surprise.

"Ax — slipped," he gasped. "Quick, Andy, off with your shirt. Tie it round my leg, above the wound, tight as you can."

Wordlessly, the boy slipped out of his shirt, knelt swiftly by his father's side, and wrapped the garment around the injured leg. Tugging with all his strength, he pulled the sleeves together tightly, then knotted them firmly.

Fear shone in the boy's eyes. "Does it hurt mightily, Father?"

Nate Folger twisted his head to look at his son. He gritted his teeth. "Yes, Andy, it pains real bad. You skedaddle over to Thad Byers' place and tell him I've had an accident. Hurry, lad!"

Andy was on his feet before his father had finished speaking. He glanced wildly about him. Jake was still hitched to a log and the old horse was not good for much more than a walk at his best. The Byers' farm was at least four miles away. The boy realized immediately that the only way to get help was to make a run for it. He was off like a shot, turning only for a final glimpse of his father. Nate Folger sat stolidly, still gripping his leg and watching his son with glazed eyes, even as a dark, crimson stain began to spread over the tourniquet.

Ignoring the half-semblance of a trail, Andy plunged recklessly through the underbrush. He found himself racing across an occasional meadow, fording the small, serpentine brook time after time. Twice he stumbled and fell as vines caught at his feet. Once he lost his footing on a small embankment, tumbled haphazardly down its side. Cut and bruised, he pulled himself to his feet and went lurching on.

Knowingly, Andy tried to steel himself to parcel his strength by slowing down, but the terror in his heart would not let him. The first two miles were torment and every step that followed sheer misery. His legs felt weighted with lead and breath was squeezed painfully from his lungs. Hope of reaching help had all but left him when the Byers' cabin swam into his line of vision across a clearing. Veering forward on legs that almost refused to support him, he was nearly across the clearing when they gave way entirely. Even then, Andy continued to crawl forward. He was shaking hysterically as Thad Byers pulled him to his feet.

"Father — " he panted brokenly. "Father — hurt bad."

The big man swung into action swiftly and soundlessly, running toward his barn. Returning with his horse, he swung the boy up behind him and in one smooth motion started off at a gallop.

Minutes seemed an eternity to Andy, even though he was conscious that they were all but flying through the woods. The silence became ominous as they neared the cabin site. Andy gave a sharp cry as he saw his father lying motionless, the ground around him stained a dark red. Byers dismounted rapidly, felt the limp wrist carefully. Slowly he removed his jacket and placed it over the still figure.

Even now, lying in his hammock on the *Enterprise* off the North African coast, Andy could recall exactly how his mother had received the news. She had come running to meet them, her face white and strained, and when Thad Byers broke the tidings —gruffly, yet tenderly—Andy thought his mother would faint.

"I'm sorry, Mother," the boy had sobbed. "If only I'd tied the shirt tighter. I tried, but I just couldn't tie it so tight as a growed man might have done."

Jen Folger had clutched her son to her, running her fingers through his hair and whispering over and again, "Lord, Thy will be done."

Days later, after she had regained her composure, his mother spoke plainly and firmly. "Andy, I want you to put aside the notion that you were at fault in any way. You did the best you could, more than any of us had a right to expect. I don't believe it would have made any difference how tightly you had tied that shirt. You know how your father prided himself on keeping his tools sharp. I'm afraid the cut was too deep for anything to have helped."

Listening to his mother's voice, Andy still had found it difficult to believe that his father was gone, that he would never hear the deep, booming laugh again, never feel the heavy friendly hand on his shoulder. He remembered Nate Folger's stories about the War of Independence, when he had served with the Massachusetts militia and had caught a piece of British steel in his leg. Nate had carried a slight limp from that time on. That small, jagged bit of steel, resting in Andy's pocket, had been a reminder that his father had come safely through the war, safely through jousts with Indians and with more than one wild animal, only to be felled by his own ax.

Dimly, he had realized that his mother was still speaking. "Andy, we'll have to face the fact that the two of us can't work the farm. It would be too much for us and I'm afraid we would be unequal to the struggle. It isn't easy to pick up and leave after all these years, but I've decided to sell the farm and move to Boston. I've friends there and I believe that I can use a thread and needle well enough to keep a roof over our heads and some food on the table as well."

Even though he had been expecting some such announcement, his mother's decision had come as a shock. It had meant giving up old Jake, their cows and their cabin—the only home he had ever known. Boston! The very mention had made Andy shiver with supressed excitement, overshadowed by vague fears. Pittsfield was the largest town he had ever seen and those who had been there said that Boston was many, many times as large, filled with wonders and strange sights beyond the imagination of a country lad. Yet, if his mother were brave enough to carve out a new life in the city, he would rather die than show his hesitancy.

Boston at the turn of the century had been a revelation. Andy gaped in open-mouthed amazement at the massive buildings that soared into the sky, at the majestic statehouse, the shops and stores, and especially at the throngs of people. Everywhere one looked, everywhere one turned, there were people of every shade, shape, and description — more people than Andy had dreamed were in existence. And the harbor — *there* was something special! Andy drew a deep breath when for the first time he saw that vast array of sails, the crush of small craft, the sturdy fishing boats and, towering above the others, the graceful clipper ships bound for China, the Mediterranean, and other strange ports throughout the world. Viewed in one colorful array, the scene was enough to make a boy's head spin.

However, as Andy soon found out, there were those who would jar him back to reality very quickly. During his first week in the city, while on an errand to the provisioner's, he found himself on a strange street, hopelessly confused about which way to go. He hesitated to inquire directions from three youths lounging near some empty barrels. However, they were the only ones in sight and he had to reach the shop and return home by nightfall.

"Can you tell me how to get to Beacon Street?" mimicked the leader of the trio, a rough-looking lad in his teens, after Andy had voiced a timid question.

"Why, certainly," mocked a second, flashing his companions a quick glance. "You go this way, bumpkin."

The shove was unexpected. Andy didn't even see the foot the third youth shoved in front of him until he was flying through the air. He landed hard on the cobblestone, nearly knocking the wind from his chest, but he bounced to his feet swiftly.

"No, you go this way," grunted the leader, giving Andy a stiff jolt on the shoulder that spun him round again.

Quick anger fled before overpowering fear as Andy went down a second, then a third time. A sharp pain flashed through the shoulder that had smashed against the stones. Rough hands yanked at his shirt pockets and, though Andy squirmed like a trapped animal, other hands pinned him firmly.

"Fast now," one of them whispered. "Someone's coming up the street."

There was a final jerk, followed by a ripping sound, and Andy's coins were gone. One last blow, a kick to the ribs, and his tormentors were fleeing down the narrow street, their footsteps mingling with raucous laughter.

The two men who helped Andy to his feet fell back a pace. Hair matted, shirt torn, face streaked with grime and tears, a rapidly swelling goose egg on his forehead, the boy might inspire pity but not familiarity. When Andy had managed to stem the flow of his tears, the men gave him directions, clearly and slowly, so that he could find his way home again. They even walked with him to the corner to make certain the trio was not lying in wait for him.

"Pack of ruffians," muttered one of the men. "It's getting so no one is safe to walk the streets of Boston without the chance of being set upon. A good caning might make those cowards change their tune."

His chin was trembling, but Andy contained his feelings until he reached the lodgings where he and his mother occupied a room. When he saw her, however, he broke into fresh tears. Holding him during the long, racking sobs, his mother patted the thin shoulder blades through the torn shirt and her eyes grew moist. It was a long moment before Andy could bring himself to tell her what had happened.

"They stole our money too," he concluded miserably.

Jen Folger took her son by the shoulders. "Andy," she said, "you've learned that the forest isn't the only dangerous place in the world. Wherever you go, you'll find that there are cowards and bullies. You'll find, too, that most folks are kindly and decent. Happily for all of us, there are a lot more of those folks than there are bullies. It's too bad about the money, of course, because we need it badly, but it's just as well you found out the hard way that it takes both kinds to make the world go round.

"Next time, though," she continued, "remember that you are your father's son. Nate fought the British and the Indians and never gave an inch. If you're set upon again, you fight back hard and fair."

His mother smiled at him. "That is, if they're not twice your size," she added. "Now let's get you washed up, mended, and ready for supper."

Andy flushed again at the knowledge that even his mother thought he might be a coward. It wasn't that he hadn't wanted to fight back; he simply had been unable to do so. Some hidden terror had seemed to grip him until he had just one desire — to flee from danger, real or imaginary.

There were other fights from time to time, but, as Andy learned his way about the city and about the ways of Boston boys (plus learning the best shortcuts to dodge a possible encounter), there were fewer and fewer scrapes. Even so, life in the city was not easy and food was far less plentiful than it had been on the farm. In addition to her sewing, Jen Folger took in washing, but without being told, Andy could see that their small supply of cash was dwindling. He was aware, too, of the strain in his mother's eyes as her needle dipped and flashed by candlelight, oftentimes long after he had taken to his bed.

And so it was with deep pride that one day he announced he had secured a job. "Mother," he said excitedly, "I've found work. Tomorrow morning I start delivering for Scott & Sons. Firewood in the winter and eggs and fruit in the summer. And you'll never guess — I'm to get a half-dollar every week!"

The work of toting and hauling toughened the slender youth's muscles and the money came in handy, but, best of all, it gave Andy an opportunity to explore the city as he ran his errands. Occasionally, his route took him past the harbor. On those days deliveries were apt to be a trifle late, even though he speeded up afterwards to make up for lost time.

The ships in the harbor were a source of endless fascination and an infrequent view of a frigate or man-o-war was enough to send shivers up and down his spine. Sitting on the quay one afternoon, legs dangling over the side, basket of eggs all but forgotten, Andy told himself for the twentieth time that the great war with England actually had started right here. True, they had signed the Declaration of Independence at Philadelphia, but it was here that the famous Boston Tea Party had taken place. It was here that the British man-o-war, the *Somerset*, had been anchored that fateful night in April, 1775, just before the battle of Lexington and Concord.

Andy had heard the story from his father so many times that he knew it by heart. Viewing the scene before him now, he could hear his father's voice once more.

"Yes, laddie," Nate Folger would say. "The men of Massachusetts were in an angry mood and the British soldiers quartered at Boston knew it only too well. They knew that the colonists were storing powder and shot, along with tools and food supplies at Concord. General Gage figgered as how it mightn't be a bad idea for him to destroy those supplies and then maybe pick up Sam Adams and John Hancock over at Lexington to put a stop on their tongues.

"Only thing was, our lads had an idea the general might be thinking along those lines and they didn't want to see their powder destroyed or have two of the best men in New England fall into the hands of the Redcoats. Paul Revere, Billy Dawes, and a score of others made it their business to keep an eye on the British, just in case they made a move.

"Long about the middle of April, they noticed a sudden bustle among the British troops stationed in the city and uncommon activity on board the *Somerset*. From the commotion of troops, and by picking up a word here and there, they learned that the British were planning a surprise move against Concord. Trouble was, they didn't know which way the Redcoats would attack. If they took Roxburg Road, it meant they would leave Boston by land. If they planned on using the Charlestown road, they'd go by water.

"Most everybody went to bed that night same as usual, not knowing the British were up to anything special, but some of the colonists were considerable more active than the Redcoats supposed. If the British left by way of Roxburg Road, Billy Dawes was to sound the alarm; if by Charlestown, Paul Revere had his work cut out for him. As everybody knows, the signal was pure and simple, a lantern in the tower of old North Church. Or, as I should say, two lanterns. One if by land, two if by water.

"Revere, he rowed over to Charlestown and waited on the shore. It was a long wait and he must have been shivering a-plenty, even though it was a spring evening. The hours passed slow, but then about eleven o'clock, he saw a single light showing in the tower. A minute passed, maybe, and then there was a second faint light gleaming across the water. Paul Revere, he was off like a ball fired out of a musket.

"You know how he roused the countryside, waking every farm and village. Thanks to that warning, there were sixty or seventy

Minutemen blocking their passage, guns in hand, by the time the Redcoats reached Lexington Green. When our lads refused to give ground, the British commander ordered his men to fire. Eight Minutemen went down for good and ten others were wounded, the very first to fall in the War for Independence.

"The British pushed on to Concord, but when they got there, the stores had disappeared. The Redcoats set the courthouse on fire and stove in the few supplies they could find, but if they thought that the colonists had given up, they were in for another surprise. Nearly four hundred Minutemen had gathered by then, and they met the British head-on at Concord Bridge. Our boys didn't march out orderly-like, or in column like the Redcoats were used to, but made their attack Indian style. Working their way behind trees, walls, and any cover they could find, they began peppering the British with ball and shot until the Redcoats ran for their very lives.

"General Gage, he sent out reinforcements soon as he heard what was up, nearly twelve hundred men with two cannon. They met up with the retreating Redcoats at Lexington. But more and more colonials were swarming up to join the Minutemen and even with cannon, the British couldn't take their marksmanship. Before long, the Redcoats were on their way back to Charlestown again, with the Minutemen nipping them every step of the way. It was a rout before they could get back to the protection of the *Somerset's* guns. The British had nearly two hundred and fifty men killed or wounded. We lost eighty-eight that day in April, back in '75."

Now, looking out over the harbor, Andy could shut his eyes and almost see the British man-o-war as she must have looked that day when the British troops returned from the battle in confusion and chagrin. The boy's thoughts were far away and he was only partly conscious of the toddler playing by himself on the quay a few feet from him. Even the sudden sound of a splash failed to rouse him fully. It was only when he heard the faint gurgling sound from the water that he realized the child had disappeared over the edge.

Andy's reaction was involuntary. Later he could not remember ripping off his jacket and making the dive. He did recall the shock of the cold water closing around him, clutching at the tot's loose coat, finally getting a grip, then pushing the boy's head above water.

Paddling desperately with his feet, Andy used his free hand to grasp the boat hook someone was holding down to him. Then strong hands were lifting them from the water as two seamen pulled them to the dock. Dizzy from exertion, Andy barely heard a voice nearby saying, "The tyke's going to be all right, I tell you. He wasn't in long enough to hurt him."

Andy was eased to one side as a rapidly growing crowd gathered about the men who were working over the little boy. Through a break in the throng, he saw a woman in the uniform of a governess, wringing her hands and crying. When the youngster finally sat up, she gave a wild cry of joy. Then, when it was apparent that the boy was all right, she scooped him up and started off down the dock at a trot, still shedding tears of fright.

One of the men who had pulled them from the water stopped briefly and patted Andy on the back. "That was fast thinking, lad. Another minute and it would have been all up with the little fellow."

The excitement over, the crowd of sight-seers quickly evaporated. Andy reached down for his eggs and was startled to discover that the basket had disappeared. He gave a second start. His jacket was gone as well. Someone in the crowd had taken advantage of the confusion to slip off with both.

Recounting the day's events to Jen Folger that evening made for painful telling. "Not only did they get my jacket and the eggs," Andy sighed, "but it cost me my job as well. Old Mr. Scott was so furious that he wouldn't even listen. Said I'd caused him to lose one of his best customers and no matter what the excuse, it wasn't good enough. He said that there was no room for irresponsibility in his firm and shouted me out the door."

Andy was still mooning over Mr. Scott's anger when they were startled by a loud and rapid knocking. His mother glanced up in astonishment as Andy swung the door open. The dapper little man standing in the doorway glared at them, then pointed his cane at Andy.

"That the one? That the boy?" he asked sharply.

Now Andy could see the girl behind him, muffled in the shadows of the passage. He recognized her as the governess who had been on the dock that afternoon.

"Yes, sir," she mumbled. "That's the very lad."

CHAPTER III

THE MAN's glare changed to a beaming smile and his voice became softer. "Boy, you've given me a devil of a time. I've spent the whole afternoon and all evening hunting you to thank you for having pulled my little nephew from the bay today. Somebody told me you delivered provisions. I finally found your employer. When I told him what really had happened, Mr. Scott said he'd be only too glad to take you back."

Pausing for breath, the fidgety visitor took a quick glance about him, absorbing every detail of the sparsely furnished room. "Old Scott didn't know exactly where you lived and I must admit that I had a devil of a time finding you. Even though I've never spent much time in this particular neighborhood, that's a bad performance for a newspaperman, now isn't it?"

Andy and his mother stood dumbly, staring at this stranger who had burst into their room and overwhelmed them with his rapid, one-sided conversation.

The little man began pacing up and down the tiny room, tapping his cane to emphasize a point, "Matter of fact, I told Mr. Scott that you wouldn't be back — that he could — well, at any rate, I told him to get another boy. I said you were going to work for me at double whatever he paid you. Now, what's-your-name

— Andy — you report first thing in the morning."

He whirled around and started out the door, then stopped. "Mrs., er, Folger, you have a fine lad there. I'm very grateful for what he did today."

The two visitors were halfway down the steps before Andy caught up to them. "Thank you very much, sir, but where should I report?"

"Why, that's right," ejaculated the little man. "Forgot to tell you, didn't I? My name's Day. Benjamin Day, editor of the *Columbia-Gazette*. You report to the newspaper office at seven o'clock tomorrow morning. Our shop is just off the Common and around the corner to the right. You can't miss the sign and you won't be able to mistake the smell of the printer's ink."

Striding along in the nippy air next morning, Andy found that Mr. Day had been right on both counts. The *Gazette* sign was easily discernible and, as he opened the door to the tinkling of a bell, the smell of printer's ink flooded his nostrils.

Working for a newspaper was an unusual occupation for a country-bred boy but, as Andy discovered in the months that followed, being employed by Benjamin Day was an even stranger experience. The mystery of type, the novelty of the printing press, and the stream of visitors that wended their way in and out of the newspaper office were constant sources of interest, and listening to the voluble Mr. Day as he prepared an editorial or wrangled with his visitors opened up new vistas for Andy. The excitable editor was apt to go flying out the door to report the arrival of a clipper ship, or he might spend hours arguing about the best way to steep tea. Or he was just as likely to burst into a violent denunciation of Thomas Jefferson and the Republicans at the drop of a hat.

"You'll get used to him," old Cony, the chief printer, confided to Andy one day as they munched biscuits and jam in the back of the shop. "Some days he gets so riled up that he's apt to fire you right out the door if you so much as cough or rustle a sheet of paper. Ten minutes later he's hunting you up, pleading with you to come back to work. No doubt about it, he's easy roused but, all things considered, Ben Day is as fair a man as ever trod a Boston street and a good employer."

Andy discovered as much for himself, but he was taken aback at the editor's outbursts on the subject of politics, especially when he battled with his friend, Mr. Ned Townsend. Nearly every day the lawyer dropped into the office after lunch for a game of checkers. Regularly as rain and taxes, the game was climaxed with a lively argument about the merits of the two political parties, the Republicans and the Federalists. Even more surprising to the boy was the fact that although they nearly came to blows, the two men would shake hands and smile when it came time for parting. Working in the shop, it was almost impossible not to overhear their heated conversation, particularly when it rose in volume.

"Ned," the little editor would exclaim. "Let me tell you it was a sad day for this nation when Tom Jefferson and the Republicans came to power. Now he's throwing Federalists out of office right and left, getting rid of the only men who could have saved our government. Theodore Dwight, the brother of Yale's president, had it right last week when he said at New Haven that 'our country is governed by knaves and blockheads.' I'm going to print that story on the front page of our newspaper. In fact, I may publish it several weeks in a row, just to let our readers know what sort of folks we have running things at Washington."

"Ben," returned his portly visitor, "you have got things slightly mixed. Throwing those misfits out of office was the best day's work Tom Jefferson ever did. If anybody's going to put our Ship of State on the right track, Mr. Jefferson is the man to do it."

Feeling the heat of battle rising, Andy edged cautiously toward the back of the shop, just in case any flying objects should hurtle through the air.

"Save our Ship of State!" shouted the editor. "Speaking of ships, just look at what he's done to our Navy. Cut it to the bone, that's what he's done, right at a time when New England needs it most. Jefferson lets the Barbary Pirates bowl over our merchantmen like tenpins, capture our tars, and throw them into dungeons while he squanders away our hard-earned taxes on some of the silliest projects imaginable. That's what we get for electing a Virginian instead of a solid New Englander."

"Seems to me you've got things more twisted than usual," growled his checker partner. "Didn't Jefferson appoint Levi Lincoln of Massachusetts as his Attorney General? Didn't he name Henry Dearborn of Maine for Secretary of War? And, as far as electing a Virginian President, I guess maybe you've forgotten General Washington was from Virginia too!"

The little printer wagged his finger fiercely. "That's beside the point. You still haven't answered my objections about the President whittling away our Navy at the very time we should be building it up. Maybe you've forgotten, but not two months ago Jefferson wrote to Samuel Smith saying he'd be disappointed if he couldn't lay up seven men-o-war in the Potomac with 'but one set of plunderers to watch over them. . .high and dry under cover from the sun.' To me, that sounds more like Queen Elizabeth's plan to keep ships of the Royal Navy from the seas so that their paint would not be damaged.

"Here we have less than a dozen ships in our whole Navy, with only a few first-class frigates such as the *Constitution, Constellation,* and the *United States,* and Jefferson wants to lay up the lot of them in the Potomac to crumble in the sun. Does that make sense to you — at the very time when the corsairs are rattling the saber and when the British are apt to impress our seamen at the flap of a sail? I tell you that Jefferson and his rattle-brained Swiss toymaker, Albert Gallatin, will founder us if things are allowed to go on as is. Why, they'd rather pay tribute to the brigands than serve them up a few cannon balls."

Moving resolutely into battle, Mr. Day's visitor shoved aside the checkerboard, his deep voice gaining in power. "Benjamin Day, you are the stubbornest man I know and possibly the least-informed person in Boston! It is true that Jefferson has tried to keep peace with the corsairs by paying them with cash and gifts. But so do all the other countries, including France and England, and they're a lot more powerful than we are. Sometimes buying peace is less expensive than sending squadrons to the ends of the earth."

Mr. Townsend paused for breath. "Another thing you seem to have forgotten is that Mr. Jefferson didn't start the business of sending tribute to the pirates. After we defeated England in the War of Independence, it meant that British men-o-war stopped protecting our merchantmen as they had done in earlier years. If you'll just jog your memory a bit, Ben, you'll recall that back in 1793, the Algerian corsairs captured eleven U.S. merchantmen in one month, along with over one hundred of our seamen.

"You may recall, too, the sort of treaty we made with Algeria in 1796, requiring us to send them twenty-one thousand dollars of naval stores every year. Why, the cost of that treaty alone, along with ransoming the captives, came to almost a million dollars.

Surely those things happened long before Mr. Jefferson took office."

The lawyer held up his hand to stave off any interruption by the editor. "I can't say that I like the idea of sending tribute to those fellers any better than you do, but Jefferson and his cabinet have a lot more on their hands than the North African brigands. Granted, Europe is at peace at the moment, but who knows when or where Napoleon will decide to strike again? Who knows what England is up to or when she may be ready to tackle France once more? I tell you, Ben, Jefferson is on the right track. Folks will let us alone if we let them alone. Meantime, Albert Gallatin has set himself a hard course to reduce our national debt. That Swiss toymaker, as you call him, has chosen an unpopular course, but it's the sort of medicine this country needs right now."

The argument ended abruptly as Mr. Townsend yanked his watch from his vest pocket.

"I'm late," he said brusquely. "I'll have to hurry back to my office if I expect to get anything done today."

The editor shoved away the checkerboard disgustedly, not bothering to retrieve the checkers that fell to the floor. "All right, Ned, if that's the way it is. You stop by tomorrow afternoon and we'll have another game. Maybe, then, I can get in the last word for a change."

The little man's belligerence had vanished as he held out his hand, smiling sheepishly. With an equally sheepish air, the lawyer grasped it. Sighing with relief, Andy and the others settled back to their work, glad that the wordy battle had ended without the throwing of inkwells. The two men's arguments always interested Andy, yet sometimes he found himself quite disturbed by the trend of the discussion.

"Cony," he said later to the chief printer, "until I heard Mr. Day speak out, I never realized what scoundrels we have governing us at Washington."

"His feathers sure were ruffled today," grinned Cony. "But don't put too much stock in everything you hear him say — or Mr. Townsend either. Remember, lad, usually there are two sides to every story. A good many times the real answer may lie someplace in between. It can't be good for their bile or liver, but I've never seen two men who enjoyed arguing politics more than that pair. Sometimes I think they'd rather miss dinner than they would their game of checkers and squabble. Too, I've a hunch that each of 'em learns more from these squalls than they'd be willing to admit. It gives each of 'em a different slant on things and shows 'em that neither of them has the complete solution, no matter how positive they pretend to be."

The printer paused as he applied a gob of black ink to his press. "But there's a heap to what Ben Day says about paying tribute to that pack of pirates. You can be sure we're never going to get those brigands off our backs simply by sending them naval stores, gunpowder, and good American dollars. The more they get, the more they'll want. Then they're certain to turn on us the first chance they get. Sure, we made treaties with Morocco in '86, with Algeria in '95, Tripoli in '96, and with Tunis in 1797, but none of them have been worth the scraps of paper they were written on. We've paid the corsairs millions and we're no better off than we were before. I've nothing against President Jefferson. Like all our government leaders past and present, he's trying to do what's best for our country. But I believe he's skinning up the wrong tree if he thinks the Barbary States are going to give our merchantmen free rein in the Mediterranean because we send them trinkets."

As the months rolled by, Andy found that he enjoyed his work more and more. The job was hard and the hours long as he ran errands, swept the shop, assisted the printers, and sometimes delivered fresh papers to firms where the latest news of shipping, commerce, and government was awaited eagerly. But there was always excitement in the air. Not only was Andy made aware of almost every important development in Boston almost as soon as it occurred, but he had an opportunity to observe men and women from nearly every walk of life as they stopped by the offices of the *Columbia-Gazette*.

In addition, there was that matter of the silver dollar handed to him every Saturday morning. The extra money proved a real help in defraying expenses — rent, purchasing provisions, and, on rare occasions, it even allowed Andy and his mother to dine at one of the city's more reasonable eating establishments.

The Sabbath was free and on those days Andy attended church services with his mother. In the evenings the two of them might spend hours trying to read the newspapers the boy brought home or laboriously learning how to write.

"Learning to read and write isn't easy," Jen Folger would declare. "But then, worthwhile things seldom are. Your father and I never learned, but I vow I'll be able to do both before the two of us are finished! Anyway, I'm determined that you'll know how. I'd always hoped that you could have some kind of book learning, but since that isn't possible, we'll just have to work it out ourselves."

As Andy soon found out, learning to write was an especially arduous task, but after months of practice both Andy and his mother were agreeably surprised to discover that they were at last beginning to get the hang of it. Mrs. Folger was delighted with the precision and clarity of her son's penmanship.

On Sundays, when his mother visited with friends or took tea with other members of the church, Andy was left to his own devices. Depending upon the season, he might take his crude ice skates and seek out one of the city's frozen ponds, watch a stick-ball game, a hurling match, or a bowling contest. At other times he was more than content to spend an afternoon at the harbor, sitting on the dock and watching the colorful array of ships from all over the civilized world. He had never had opportunity to set foot on board one of them, but as he watched the sails of a trim schooner billowing in the breeze as she slipped neatly out of the harbor, he ardently hoped that someday he might.

Meanwhile, life at the *Columbia-Gazette* continued with its pulsating flow of excitement, checker games, and political arguments. Judging from the intensity of the latter, Andy gathered that the Barbary corsairs were growing bolder in their attacks on American merchantmen and that New England ship owners were taking a gloomy view of the entire proceedings. Apparently, fewer and fewer American ships dared risk the highly profitable North African run.

Even so, Andy was taken by surprise one morning when Benjamin Day bounced into his office without bothering to close the door behind him and angrily slammed a packet of papers on his desk.

"Now they've done it!" he exploded to the world in general. "Listen to these reports! Not only are the corsairs allowed to sweep the seas of our merchantmen, but now they make our men-o-war eat humble pie as well. Word has arrived that the Dey of Algeria actually pressed the *George Washington* into his service to carry gifts and Algerian envoys to the Sultan of Turkey! Just imagine! The first United States warship ever to enter the Mediterranean—forced to become a messenger scow for the Algerians.

"I'm not blaming Captain Bainbridge," Ben Day continued to the small audience that had gathered in the doorway. "Heaven only knows the humiliation that young ship commander must have suffered. What I am saying is that instead of having one frigate there to protect our shipping, we should have had a squadron, able to blow the Dey into the next world if he so much as gave us a cross look. Only thing those pirates understand!"

Later, the chief printer pieced together the story for Andy.

"Ben is right," Cony said. "It wasn't Captain Bainbridge's fault, far as I can see. Seems that after he'd anchored the *George Washington* off Algiers, the Dey sent word he'd be right pleased if Bainbridge would tote some gifts, supplies, and Algerian envoys over to Constantinople. Old Mustafa, he seems to have had the idea that anyone who is paying him tribute as we do should be only too glad to run a few errands to boot.

"There wasn't much Cap'n Bainbridge could do, I guess, what with the *Washington* anchored right under the shore batteries of Algiers and the Dey just itching to get his fingers on some of our fat merchantmen sitting out in the harbor. Not only that, but Mustafa made him haul down the Stars and Stripes and fly the Algerian flag instead. So Bainbridge takes the ambassadors and their presents on board and delivers 'em to the Sultan about two months later."

The printer smiled at Andy. "It must have been some sight, at that. According to our reports, the Algerians loaded on horses, cattle, over a hundred head of sheep, and a batch of parrots, in addition to a lot of fancy fabrics and passengers. A motley collection for an American man-o-war! Captain Bainbridge's hands were tied, what with all those merchantmen just sitting around waiting to be picked off like fat geese, but he didn't altogether take it lying down. He yanked down the Dey's flag once he cleared the harbor, and sent up Old Glory again."

Cony's voice became sober as he added, "Only thing is, it's bound to stir up more trouble for us, in addition to humiliating our Navy. Tripoli, Tunis, Morocco, and Algiers, too — they're like a pack of vultures. They're apt to jump in and battle for the pickings any time they figure a country's too weak to stand 'em off. It's near certain tribute alone will never keep 'em satisfied. Just two years ago we shipped twenty-six barrels of silver dollars to the Dey. Now he turns one of our frigates into a menagerie for lions and tigers, or a scow for sheep and cattle. Not very thankful of him, is it?

"Nope, Andy," the old printer concluded gloomily, "it looks to me as how the next move is up to us."

Partly because of his job at the newspaper, and somewhat because of his growing interest in anything that sailed, Andy followed every scrap of news about American shipping in the Mediterranean and kept a keen ear tuned to any information that Ben Day might volunteer on the subject. Oftentimes, Andy's conversations with his mother slipped around to events taking place off Africa.

Jen Folger would gently try to switch the talk to other matters. "Algeria, Tripoli, Tunis — sometimes I wonder if there really are such places. If there are, I'm sure they're much too far away for us to bother our heads about. Now, Andy, tell me what work was like today."

At other times, however, she remained silent, her fingers flashing skillfully as her needle darted in and out of whatever garment she might be sewing. She sometimes stole a troubled glance at her son as he talked about men-o-war, what President Jefferson had said, or what the corsairs might be up to. One summer evening when Andy brought home especially disturbing news, she knew the decision she dreaded was not far off.

"Mother," the boy sputtered, "Tripoli has declared war on the United States. It happened last May, but word just reached Boston today. They say that the Pasha felt the Algerians and other pirates were getting more than their share of tribute from us. When we refused to boost the value of his gifts, he simply whacked down our consul's flag mast and called for war. But even before the news reached Washington, President Jefferson had sent a squadron of ships to the Mediterranean. Maybe now those Barbary brigands will get a good look at American fighting tars."

Eying her son, Jen Folger was reminded of a fidgety, long-legged colt. Tall for his age and too long for his sleeves, he pranced about the room, adam's apple working convulsively as he told her what the U.S. Navy would do to the enemy.

"Andy," she chided gently after awhile. "Slow down to a gallop. I don't like to see you get yourself so worked up about all these things in far-off lands. Just remember that these are none of our doings and that you're a boy, not the captain of a battle cruiser. I wish that Mr. Day wouldn't carry on so about politics and war."

"But Mother," replied the boy quickly, "it *does* concern us. When the Pasha of Tripoli declares war on the United States, then he declares war on you and me, along with everyone else in Boston and throughout our nation. If he should whip us in the Mediterranean, Mr. Day says it would affect all our shipping and commerce. If he should whip us, it might lead England, France or Spain to try their hand against us if we look like easy picking from the kettle."

Nonetheless, Andy faltered under his mother's questioning

gaze. With effort, he told her how old Cony had fallen into a pond while fishing and had caught a bad cold from his adventure. Watching his mother ease her chair around to gain additional light for her sewing from the candle on the table, he saw how weary her eyes looked, even as her needle and thread continued their swift, steady movement. Without any need for putting it into words, he was reminded how much she needed him here at home.

As the weeks turned into months and fall eased toward winter, Andy became even more conscious of his obligation to his mother and how important his weekly wage was in helping to pay for their food and lodging. Despite this knowledge, despite the fear that lurked deep within him, there was a hunger in his heart to be part of the exciting events that were taking place abroad, a yearning that could not be denied. One day that feeling reached a climax as Benjamin Day returned from a visit to the shipping offices.

Stamping the snow from his boots and shaking droplets from his greatcoat, the editor sat down wearily at his battered desk.

"Well, wouldn't that freeze your fingers?" he said to Cony. "This morning one of the ship owners told me that our great adventure against the Barbary States has amounted to almost nothing. Here we've been at war with Tripoli for nearly a year and we have hardly anything to show for it."

"Why, I thought our tars and marines were doing first rate," Cony exclaimed in a surprised voice.

"Oh, they would, if given the chance," replied the little man bitterly. "It's just that we haven't prosecuted the war with vigor. Jefferson did send some men-o-war over there, and that was all to the good. As you know, he dispatched the frigates *President, Philadelphia,* and *Essex*, along with the schooner *Enterprise,* all under the command of Commodore Richard Dale, 'way last May. Trouble is, he made them a squadron of observation only.

"You know how Jefferson is," Mr. Day continued. "Takes every word of the Constitution as his bible and holds that under that document only Congress can declare war. That's why he ordered the squadron to act strictly on the defensive. Under those orders, Commodore Dale wasn't even allowed to take prizes, had just to maintain a blockade. I guess you remember Dale was once John Paul Jones' favorite lieutenant. You can bet he would have made the fur fly if given half a chance."

Benjamin Day banged his fist on the desk. "Only thing that happened in the whole year was that the *Enterprise* caught up with a Tripolitan man-o-war and whipped her neatly. Since he couldn't take her as a prize, Captain Sterett dismantled her of everything but a spar and sail and sent her home. When Dale's cruise was up, he left the *Philadelphia* to blockade Tripoli under Captain Barron. They say Barron showed up off the enemy harbor just once, and then only for a few hours. I tell you, Cony, we're the laughing stock of the Barbary nations. In confidence, I can tell you also that insurance rates on merchantmen are rising again.

"There's one ray of hope, though." The newspaper editor's face brightened. "Congress has declared war officially at last and they're getting ready a second squadron to visit the Mediterranean. Now maybe something will happen!"

Andy, who had been listening to the conversation as he swept the pressroom floor, felt his pulses quicken. A second squadron! He was older now, and stronger too. If only he dared ask his mother's consent to enlist! He was certain that his father had not held back a day when the War for Independence had begun, had responded boldly to the first call for volunteers. If only he dared—

Later in the day he pressed Cony for full details of the new squadron.

"I don't know why you should get so all-fired up about it, Andy," drawled the printer. "I hear that Jefferson is sending the *Chesapeake* as flagship, the *Adams, New York,* the *John Adams,* and *Constellation.* The *Enterprise* will make her second trip over there too. And we've still got the *Philadelphia, Boston, Essex,* and *George Washington* on station in the Mediterranean. Even though a few of those are due home soon, it gives us a powerful force."

Noting the eagerness with which the boy received all this, Cony continued. "Captain Thomas Truxtun, who did so well in the War of Independence, and who proved himself again in the action against the French down in the West Indies — he was slated to lead the squadron. They were short on captains and they wanted Truxtun to command his own flagship, the *Constellation,* as well. Maybe you don't know it, lad, but captains are a touchy lot. When he learned he had to do both jobs, Truxtun seems to have felt he'd had a demotion, so he turned down the whole shebang. Too bad, because he was a good man. Instead, they gave command to Commodore Richard Morris. Funny thing, they gave *him* a captain for his flagship without so much as batting an eyelash. Maybe they didn't want to risk another turn-down. Anyway, Morris, he's got some good ships under him and I'll wager that he makes the pirates jig his tune."

Listening to the printer's words, Andy felt himself irresistibly pushed toward making the announcement from which, once made, there would be no escape. Once he had told someone what he intended to do there could be no pulling back unless he wanted to risk becoming an object of ridicule.

"Cony," Andy blurted out at last, "how do you — how does one go about signing up in the Navy? I want to volunteer for that squadron!"

There was little surprise in the old man's eyes but his voice was serious as he answered, "I figgered you might have some such notion, Andy, but let me tell you that life in the Navy is no Sabbath picnic on the Common. Following the sea is a rugged life for man or boy and I've plenty of missing relatives to testify to that. Remember too, lad, that your mother depends on you.

"Still, if you're so determined that nothing else will satisfy, all you have to do is head down to the docks, visit the Navy office and scratch your name on a piece of paper. I'd better warn you, though, that they've changed the rules too. Up until lately, you signed up for a year of service. Trouble with that idea was that just about the time a ship was ready for action, half the enlistments would be up. Then they'd have to send the ship back to the States again to relieve those men from duty. Now it's for two years before the mast when you put your Andy Folger down."

Heading homeward that evening, Andy knew that the hardest part lay ahead of him. He rehearsed the speech he would make in asking his mother's consent. He'd vow to be good, say his prayers, and send her every copper of his pay. As he walked along, Andy saw in his imagination a Tripolitan pirate, a giant swarthy corsair with saber drawn, coming toward him menacingly. Suddenly fingers of fear tugged at his heart. If only he hadn't made his rash statement to Cony, if only he had thought it over until tomorrow! He groaned inwardly. The die was cast now — there was no chance of retreat.

A light snow had begun to fall and he could hear the ring of skates and cheery laughter as he passed a frozen skating pond. Ordinarily, Andy would have dawdled to watch, but tonight he had more important things on his mind. His fast walk changed to a dog trot as he neared home. He went up the front steps of the lodging house at a bound. The passageway was dim. In his hurry, he almost stumbled against one of the lodgers, old Mrs. Headley, creaking down the hall with something in her hand.

"Careful, Andrew!" she cackled. "You gave me such a start you almost made me drop this broth."

Excitedly, the elderly woman rattled on without pausing for breath. "Oh, Andrew, lad, it's a godsend you're home at last. Your mother's had a terrible fall. Terrible, terrible. I think she's broken her hip and maybe her skull as well. I wanted to send a neighor boy to fetch you from the shop, but your poor dear mother wouldn't hear of it. The doctor's in there — a terrible fall."

CHAPTER IV

WHITE WITH fear, Andy dodged swiftly past her and flung open the door to their quarters. Jen Folger was lying on the bed, hair awry, deep circles of pain under her eyes, a streak of tears across her cheeks. Disregarding the doctor, Andy moved to her side. He took a quick look at her, then buried his head on her shoulder.

"It's all right, Andy," she said softly. "Everything's going to be all right. It's not bad at all."

"Easy, lad," said the doctor, pulling him to his feet. "Your mother's right. It isn't bad at all. I've seen worse breaks at a taffy pull. Considering the spill she took, it's a wonder she didn't fracture her skull as well as her hip."

Tall and cadaverous, with a long thin nose and spectacles, the doctor looked ominous in his black professional garb, though his manner was kindly. "As breaks go, this is a nice clean one. There's a lot of pain and shock, of course, and it won't do to have you hanging all over her, but I'm certain the hip will mend firmly, given time and care."

He shook a long finger at his patient. "You do as you're told, Mrs. Folger, and we'll have you up and about in no time. I don't want you to do anything but rest for a few weeks. Then, depending on how your hip's coming along, I don't see why you can't sit up and do a little sewing, if you promise not to go bounding about."

Closing the black bag and adjusting his spectacles, the doctor gave Andy a friendly pat on the back.

"You've got a good strong lad to run your errands and do the chores while you take a much-needed rest, Mrs. Folger. Now who could ask for more than that?"

As soon as the doctor had gone, old Mrs. Headley, who had been hovering in the background, served Jen Folger the soup, then took her departure. Andy could hear her tapping all the way down the hall, muttering to herself, "Terrible, terrible."

Leaning against the door, thoughts of the ships that soon would be sailing for North Africa, as well as the speech he had rehearsed, flashed through Andy's mind. It was so easy to be selfish, he thought, so easy to forget how others might depend upon you. Then his face flushed. No matter how he attempted to disguise it, there was no denying the intense feeling of relief that flooded over him at the knowledge that now he would not be able to volunteer. Old Cony and the others — they would see that he had no other course but to remain with his mother. Much as he might like to go, it was his duty to stay behind at Boston.

Turning to his mother, he said, "Don't worry, Mother. We'll make out fine — just as the doctor said. You wait and see."

In the days that followed, shopping for provisions, carrying firewood and water, running errands, and cooking all their meals left Andy little time for thought. The news that the ships had sailed for Tripoli made little impression on his mind. His work was harder at the print shop and, at the same time, easier. Harder, because now old Cony was teaching him the rudiments of setting type by hand. Easier, because Mr. Day had hired another boy to sweep up, run deliveries, and assist in the chores of printer's devil.

Andy had never mentioned his mother's fall to Benjamin Day, although he had confided the trouble to Cony. What with more advertising, more pages to fill, and the ever-present competition provided by the other newspapers in town, the editor seemed to have his hands full. Andy doubted Mr. Day would have heard even if he'd told him of the accident. It came as a great surprise, therefore, when, a week after his mother's mishap, the paymaster handed him two dollars instead of one.

"No mistake at all," Benjamin Day said gruffly when Andy approached him. "You've done your work dependably, even though the newspaper business was strange to you. The merchants like you, the advertisers like you, and Cony tells me that you're the best help he's ever had. So we pay you what you're worth, that's all."

The editor's eyes twinkled. "After all, we've got to protect ourselves. Who knows? Maybe what's-his-name, old Scott, was just itching to hire you back at twice what we were paying you. So we beat him to it."

Jen Folger's hip mended more slowly than they had hoped but, true to the doctor's word, the bone knit firmly. Gradually she was able to sit up in bed, her leg held straight and firm in the stiff splints and heavy plaster-of-paris sleeve that had been fashioned for it.

This offered encouragement, at least. Andy suddenly realized that his mother had never uttered one word of complaint, even though he was aware how painful the inactivity must be for her. It was a great relief to them both when she was able to sit in the chair Andy had placed by the window so that she could use the sunlight to sew by and watch passersby.

When at last the doctor removed the splints, Andy's pent-up

feelings almost burst and he felt like dancing in the street.

"Easy now, Mrs. Folger," said the doctor, rubbing his chin thoughtfully as he watched her test the leg gingerly. "A few steps, that's all you can have today. But it's looking good. I see no reason why you can't exercise it by taking a few more steps each day. In fact, before too long I imagine you'll be fit to go running up and down the Common, good as new."

The burst of laughter from both mother and son produced the effect the doctor had hoped for and he left them in good humor. "Looks as though I won't be needed around here till the next time one of you tumbles down the staircase, but remember, you know where I live if you need me."

With his duties at home and in the shop, Andy had all but forgotten the corsairs. The daily checker games and political arguments between editor and lawyer had been halted because Mr. Ned Townsend had been on a business trip to New York and Washington, then had spent a long period recovering from an attack of gout. It was with a start one afternoon that the boy heard the voices of the two men raised in loud argument. He grinned to himself as he noted that the passage of time had not diminished the power of their lungs or the acidity of their tongues.

"I tell you, Ned Townsend," the editor was shouting angrily, "the gout must have gone to your head rather than your foot. I suppose you're going to tell me that we're winning the war with Tripoli because they haven't sunk our fleet," he said with thinly veiled sarcasm. "Probably you're more than pleased with the way that Jefferson has set down the corsairs."

The lawyer hesitated, then rested his arms on the table again. "No, Ben," he said gloomily, "I'm not. As you know, many of our clients have ships operating in those waters or, rather, ships that should be operating over there. What should have been settled back in 1801 turns out to be nothing but a stalemate. At that, it isn't Jefferson's fault altogether. True, maybe he hasn't prosecuted the war so vigorously as he might, but he's sent two squadrons out there and nothing much has happened. Commodore Dale never received war orders till it was time for him to return home."

The big man sighed. "Everybody hoped Commodore Morris would make the Pasha of Tripoli toe the mark. He had a powerful squadron but, with the exception of a few skirmishes, his cruise wasn't worth much, even in the way of a blockade. Then we lost more prestige when the Tripolitans captured one of our merchantmen, the *Ben Franklin,* and put her crew in irons. That cost us thirty-five thousand in round American dollars to ransom them back. Nope, old Yessef Karamanli still holds winning cards and I'm less than satisfied."

With the heat of battle diminished, the two men dropped their voices again. Working on a press near the rear of the shop, Andy strained forward to hear the rest of the conversation.

"At any rate," Mr. Townsend said, "maybe things will pick up this year. They're fitting out a third squadron and it's to be under the command of Edward Preble. I guess you know Commodore Preble is a staunch, solid New Englander and as —"

The crash of a porcelain water pitcher on the floor of the shop brought both men to their feet as Andy, leaning too far forward, tilted the vessel from a desk to its shattering end. The startled pair stared at the broken pitcher, then at the boy, now flushing in confusion.

"Egad," exclaimed the lawyer. "I'm late for a meeting with a client. I've got to get back to the office right away. See you tomorrow, Ben."

"I'm sorry about the pitcher, Mr. Day," Andy said after Mr. Townsend had departed.

"That's all right, Andy," replied the editor dreamily, eyes on the ceiling as he leaned back in his chair. "I never thought I'd see the day when Ned Townsend would agree with me about anything. No sir, I never thought I'd see the day."

The news of the third squadron of ships for Tripoli brought home to Andy his earlier dreams. Once again he was filled with an intense desire to play a part in the war, to sign into the Navy, to board a man-o-war and see the far-off lands that played such a vital role in New England shipping. Closing his eyes, he could see himself boarding a pirate ship, leading a charge of marines against the enemy. His mother's hip had now healed completely. She had more sewing jobs than she could take care of, and there was a tidy nest egg laid by. Surely now there was no excuse for not volunteering. Today, tonight — this was the time to seek her permission. Surely it was now or never.

Following supper that night, as they washed and dried the dishes his mother turned to Andy. "What's the matter with you tonight, son?" she asked. "You've been fidgety as an old rooster scratching for a fat worm. Did everything go all right at work today? Or is it something else?"

With a glance at his mother, Andy threw his carefully rehearsed speech to the winds. "Mother," he burst out, "they're assembling a third squadron for Tripoli. I simply must go with them!"

Jen Folger flinched as though she had been struck, then recovered her composure as her son babbled on. Andy's pent-up emotions came tumbling out, assailing her ears in a torrent of words.

"Don't you see, Mother?" the boy pleaded. "I'm fourteen now, older than Father was when he volunteered for the Massachusetts militia, and I'm big and strong. President Jefferson has called for men to man the ships. If you consent, I could be among them. Please, Mother, say the word. Let me sign into the Navy."

Big and strong, his mother thought, gazing tenderly at this awkward stick of a lad, the shock of unkempt brown hair curling over the large ears, the sensitive face with its brooding blue eyes now tense with eagerness. Working inside a dingy newspaper office from dawn to dusk, with little chance for fresh air and exercise, had made his thin features pale and a little drawn. Tall and gawky he might be but, to her, he would always be a baby. He was all she had.

"Andy," she sighed, "you're so young and the Navy is such a hard life. You're too young to go gallivanting half around the world by yourself, let alone fight a war against those horrible pirates."

Inwardly, the boy shivered at mention of the word, but he cast the thought aside and pressed on determinedly. "Why, Mother, I'm old as the hills. I can look Cony in the eye and I'm already taller than Mr. Day."

Jen Folger eyed her son thoughtfully. She sensed that the boy felt need to prove himself. She remembered how, even as a small child, Andy had started at the sound of a cracking branch, how he would cut and run at any threat of danger, real or imagined. She remembered the talks she had held with Nate about the boy's timidity and how she'd always said in defense of him, "Let's be patient. Given time, he'll get over his fear." But he hadn't. Fear still showed, even though she would never let him know it. It would be hard on both of them, but the lad deserved a chance to test his mettle away from her apron strings. There would be danger on the seas and even greater peril lurking off the Barbary Coast, but the world was filled with danger and sometimes it must be faced. Too, there was little doubt that the boy truly wished to serve his country as his father had done before him.

"All right, Andy," she said at last. "You have my consent. You may sign. I've seen this coming for a long time. I guess I've known you'd never be satisfied until you were part of this war against the pirates. In some ways you're a lot like your father was — more than you know — stubborn as a mule when you take an idea into your head. I'll worry while you're gone, but I'm real proud that you're going to serve our country."

Even before his mother had finished speaking, Andy flung himself into her arms. Had he been able to see her face by the dim light of the lamp, he would have seen that she fought to hold back tears. Had he been awake later that night, he might have heard her soft, nearly inaudible weeping. And had he known how close his mother had come to using the one sentence that would have held him at Boston, he might have changed his mind. But Jen Folger came from pioneer stock. She knew the lad's petition had not been tendered lightly and thus she never uttered the words that would have tied him to her side: "Andy, I need you."

A week later, listening to the creak of the oarlocks as the Navy launch moved from the dock on its way to the proud sloop riding at anchor, Andy had an inkling of how his mother must have felt during these last few days. Stealing a glance at the three other hands occupying the launch, Andy was glad that no tears had been shed at the parting on the dock.

Old Cony had stood there, tall and frail, staring soberly at the ships in the harbor. "We'll miss you at the shop, lad," he smiled. "But we'll be there when you get back. You can count on that. Take good care of yourself and don't do anything rash if you get within hailing distance of the corsairs. Take your cue from the older hands and do as they do."

To Andy's surprise, Benjamin Day was more flustered than any of the others who had come to see him off.

"I can't fathom whatever put this foolish notion into your head, running off to trade blows with the pirates," the little printer said gruffly. "But now that you've gone and signed up, let me say we're all proud of you. Our good wishes go with you. And remember, boy, there's a job waiting for you so long as you want."

The editor's voice became even gruffer. "Don't trouble your head about your mother while you're away, Andy. Rest easy that we'll look in on her while you're gone and make sure everything is all right. By the way, here's a little going-away present, one you may want to turn over to her."

When the boy and his mother moved to one side for a final moment to themselves, Andy was astonished to discover that the small packet Mr. Day had handed him contained a gold eagle — twenty dollars — nearly half as much as his father had earned from a full year's work on the farm.

His mother's voice was soft as she said, "Good-by, Andy. God bless you and keep you. Remember I'll be waiting for you here at Boston. Write to me when you've a chance — and, son, remember to keep your feet dry and your neck covered from the drafts."

Andy kissed her lightly on the cheek. It was time to go.

CHAPTER V

TURNING HIS gaze away from the Boston shore line, Andy glanced at his companions with interest. Aside from the oarsmen, there were three others sitting in the stern sheets of the launch, knee-deep in seabags and small stores. Two were young seamen being transferred from another ship to their new berth, and each was telling the other how he would soon square away their new shipmates and show them how things were done in the best sailing circles.

The third passenger, a man in his late forties or early fifties, drew Andy's closer attention. Square and stocky, with a broad brown forehead and a face as leathery as a well-cured hide, the old tar sat quietly, the stub of a black pipe held between tobacco-stained teeth, watching the pattern of the city's buildings as the shore slid away from them. Andy stared at the insignia that showed the man had served against the French fleet in 1798. Now, the resolute gray eyes looked out from under shaggy eyebrows, returning Andy's gaze.

"What's your name, lad?" the man's voice boomed, even though he spoke in a normal tone.

"Andy Folger, sir."

The stocky salt gave a low chuckle. "No, lad, you don't have to 'sir' me. I'm not an officer and never will be. My name is Ransom. John Ransom. But I've tinkered with powder and shot so long I'd never even answer if someone called me by my Christian name. Everybody on board calls me Guns."

Andy absorbed this in respectful silence until his companion spoke again. "This your first duty, lad?"

"Yes, si. . .I mean, yes, Guns," the youth stammered. "I signed my papers just the other day. This is my first assignment."

"Well, Andy," said the gunner in a friendly tone, "all the drivel and fuss of shore is behind you now. You'll find a different life out here. Not a bad life, either, if you meet it halfway. Put your mind to it. Do more listening than talking and you'll learn something.

"Naturally, every tar thinks his ship is the best in the squadron, but that's just what your new ship happens to be — the finest afloat. I've been ashore to visit my sister who lives at Boston, but let me tell you that it will feel good to get my feet back on deck again! Maybe you'll feel the same way someday. Too, I think you'll like our captain, young Lieutenant Stephen Decatur. No nonsense about him, and he knows his ships and sails, even though he's less than twenty-five years old. I served under his daddy on the *Delaware* when we tackled the French down in the Indies in '98. We're right fortunate to be serving under him — if he's only half as good as the old commodore."

Andy was about to ask a timid question when the gunner exclaimed suddenly, "There's my beauty! The finest ship afloat, the *U.S.S. Enterprise*."

Andy breathed deeply as they drew within hailing distance of his new home. Riding gently on the ebb tide, the trim triple-masted sloop was indeed a thing of beauty — from the gracefully curved bow to the tip of her mainmast — and the sight of her guns sent a shiver up the boy's spine.

"Remember," the gunner was saying, "when you reach the top of the ladder, set down your gear, turn and salute Old Glory. Then swing round and salute the officer-of-the-watch. Tell him your name, give him your papers, and he'll do the rest." Gunner Ransom grinned as he added, "And him — you'd better call him 'sir.' "

Andy spent his first hours on board ship in a daze. From the moment the officer-of-the-watch checked his papers until he finally closed his eyes that night, it seemed to him that he had been pushed, pulled, and whirled about until his head was spinning off his shoulders. All the unfamiliar faces, gruff voices, sharp commands, the new sights and strange smells, made his ears ring and his eyes blur.

"Messenger," the watch officer had said to a lad standing nearby, "here's the new cabin boy. This is his first day on board ship. Since he'll be bunking near you, I guess you'd better show him his accommodations in the forecastle. And hurry back."

Andy was too absorbed in collecting his gear to notice the quick wink the officer had given the boy. If he had he might not have placed too much credence in the admonition to hurry back.

"Sling that bag over your shoulder, younker, and let's get moving," sang out the messenger. "We move fast on this ship and you're no exception."

Andy noticed that the stocky, freckle-faced lad was no older than himself and, although he smarted at the messenger's patronizing manner, he realized that the boy was an old hand on shipboard. Even if Andy had felt like snapping back a retort, it would have been difficult as he struggled under the burden of his seabag.

"You're sure to like our quarters, Folger," grinned the boy. "When they learned you were going to be on board this voyage, they fitted us out with big bunks and feather mattresses. And as for space, we live in style. Not even the first lieutenant's cabin can compare with ours."

Intent on trying to follow the nimble youth as the messenger skipped easily over blocks, chocks, cleats, and running lines, Andy made no reply. The stocky messenger was in a hurry and kept up such a steady pace that Andy had to scurry to keep up with him. Up ladders and down, through hatches and around winches they went, the Boston boy huffing and puffing to keep up with his guide who never ceased his steady flow of chatter.

"You'll want to watch out for Cook, though," the boy said as they rounded a corner. "Billy Blossom has the sharpest temper of any man in the squadron and since you'll be working direct for him, you'll have to keep an eye peeled for the danger signs. When you see him wearing his cook's hat cocked over to one side, that's fair warning he's in a temper and working up to a squall. You never can tell what will set him off, either. One is the mention of Boston. Never say that word in his presence or he's apt to fly into a rage. They say that's 'cause he lost a duel there. Well, not exactly 'lost' the duel, at that. Just wounded his man instead of killing him outright. But to Billy Blossom, that's the same as losing."

The messenger waited for Andy to gain the top of another ladder before he went on, "Another thing to watch out for and that's his name. Maybe it's just another of his superstitions, but he doesn't allow anyone to call him by his right name, Blossom. He wants all of us to call him Petal and that's what we do. Matter of fact, that's what happened to the last mess boy. One day he got excited in the galley and forgot."

"What did the cook do to him?" Andy asked, a bit breathlessly.

"Got him with a cleaver. Not bad, though, because when the doctor finished sewing him up, they found he still had two fingers on that hand. With a little practice, they say he may make a fine two-fingered seaman someday. Naturally, they couldn't let him stay on board because no one could tell when Cook might fly at him again. They say the captain would like to get rid of Cook — transfer him to another ship because he's wounded so many of our crew, but since the captain's right crazy about the way Blossom — I mean Petal — fries apple fritters, he just can't bear to let him go. Sometimes, though, I wish he would because Cook is so unpredictable. Lookee there, Folger, at what I got last week when I didn't move swift enough."

Holding out his hand, the messenger showed Andy a shallow cut, now nearly healed, but still looking raw.

"I didn't move quick enough," added the boy ruefully. "I'd made the mistake of just mentioning I had some friends at Boston before I remembered. Blossom came down with his knife, just grazing me there. You can bet I moved after that. I got out of that galley like lightning. Just in time, too, because the knife he flung at me went into the door a half-inch deep. If it hadn't been for that good old door between us, Sam Plummer wouldn't be here today."

Tripping, sliding, and sweating to keep pace, Andy strained to hear more of the ferocious cook who would be his immediate superior. He shuddered at the thought of the long knife quivering in the door. He began to wonder about life in the Navy. It might have been less exciting on land, but certainly it was less dangerous at — He caught himself just in time. He had nearly uttered that fatal word, Boston.

"Life's hard at sea," the freckle-faced youth continued as they walked along. "But then, the good food more than makes up for it. Tasty biscuits twice a day and all the water you can drink — except when we run short and it's rationed to a mouthful or so a day. Then on Sundays, maybe a big bowl of bean soup and any tea that's left over from the officers' mess. Oh, we eat royal all right. Why, I remember one Sabbath just a few months ago — "

"Say!" interrupted Andy suspiciously as they popped out of a hatch. "Didn't we come this way once before?

"Well, you are a landlubber," replied his guide smartly. "Don't you know all ladders and hatches look alike? We're not going so direct as we might because we're not allowed to go through officers' country or use the quarterdeck."

Andy accepted this answer, but he was suddenly sure he had passed a certain deck cleat before, a cleat he had tripped over not once but twice. Too tired and bewildered to voice another protest, he also realized that he still needed the guide to find his quarters.

"Here we are," the boy said cheerily at last. "Safe and sound in our good old snuggery."

Andy glanced at his surroundings in dismay. Located in a dark, dank little corner, lighted only partially by an oil lamp, there was scarcely enough room to turn around, let alone store any gear. Dismayed, Andy dropped his seabag to the deck and sat upon it, breathing deeply to regain his wind.

"Where do I — where do we sleep?" he asked weakly.

In reply, the boy pointed to two tightly rolled hammocks strung between two stanchions. "There's our good old bunks. Mine is the lower. Yours will be the upper."

Andy's protest was feeble. "But you said we had feather mattresses and more room than the first lieutenant."

"Why, that's so," remarked the boy easily. "I did. 'Course that was just a figure of speech. What I should have said was that they're as comfortable as featherbeds. And as for room, you've never seen so much room outside of a Virginia mansion. Oh, it's a royal lodging. Now you take that other mess boy — the one who lost his fingers. He didn't have it so good. He had to sleep on a cask head, and when he got up for watch or duty in the galley, it almost hurt to listen to him creak as he tried to unknot himself."

"But where will I store my things?" wailed Andy.

"Folger," the mess boy said, "you brought enough gear to outfit the whole squadron. You'll learn that space on board ship is precious. You take the room a landsman has to throw his clutter around in, divide that by five, then subtract a few, and you'll make real good use of what space is left. Any tar worth his salt can pack all his gear in his shirt pocket and still have room for his tobacco or comb, depending on which he values most. I've got to scoot now, but when I'm off duty I'll come back and take you down to the galley. We sail tomorrow and there's a lot to do."

It seemed only a little while to Andy before the freckle-faced lad once more bounced down the ladder and was at his side again. While he waited for him Andy had ventured out of the cubbyhole and had peeked into the main section of the forecastle where the crew lived. What Sam Plummer had said was true. It was almost empty now, for most of the hands were topside, working in the rigging or standing watch, and only a few men were in the compartment. But judging from the cramped quarters, from the hammocks tied neatly one above the other and arranged in a quadrangle around a rough-hewn wooden table, there was little room for aught but breathing. And from the stuffy odor of old tobacco, unwashed clothing, and the lingering smell of unwashed bodies, even breathing well might be difficult at times.

"Now's our chance to slip down to the galley," young Plummer told Andy. "Let's hope we find Cook in good humor."

Andy eased into the galley as though he were treading on eggs.

His first glimpse of the reputedly fierce little cook was not reassuring. The man's hat was cocked to one side of his head, just as Sam had warned, and the round little eyes were snapping wrathfully. Andy's own eyes were drawn like a magnet to the long thin knife with which the cook was peeling potatoes so deftly.

"So this is the new mess boy, is it?" Blossom said angrily. "Took you long enough to report on board, boy, and us short-handed, too. I hope you're not a hopeless case, lad. Last time they sent us a cabin boy who couldn't tell port from starboard after six months at sea. I don't know what those lunkheads on shore are up to. In fact, sometimes I wonder whose side they're on — ours or the corsairs. Where are you from, boy?"

Andy stared, mesmerized by the circles in the air the cook was making with his knife as he sputtered and growled.

"Oh, glory!" groaned the cook, as Andy stood silent. "Now they've sent me one that can't talk. Where do you live, boy?"

Brought back to earth by the repeated question, Andy began a quick reply. "Why, I'm from Bos — why, er — from Massachusetts, sir."

"Massachusetts, eh? Massachusetts where?"

Andy colored as he eyed the circling knife. "Well, sir, I'm from right around — er — well, I was born right near West Pittsfield in the Connecticut Valley."

"Tarnation!" snapped the little man. "He knows where he was born but he doesn't know where he lives. Oh well, maybe everything isn't lost if he can learn to carry a pot of tea up to the wardroom on a wet night. Sam, you take him topside and get him out from under my feet. I've got a lot to do and there's no use breaking him in until we're underway."

At the door, Andy turned and spoke again, "Thank you, sir. It's been very nice to meet you, Mr. Petal."

He had just time to see the cook's face slowly grow livid. He started toward Andy, knife in hand, then Sam was pushing Andy up the ladder.

"Quick, Folger," the messenger burst out. "Up you go! It's one of his spells."

After the two boys were gone, the cook regained his composure and returned to peeling potatoes. "That's a strange one for you," he mused to himself. "Sending me a lad who doesn't know where he lives and who has the gall to call me Petal!" A slow grin spread over his face. "Petal indeed," he thought. "The very name that riles me most — the name the crew only dares to call me behind my back!"

Topside, Andy was getting his wind again. The encounter with the excitable cook had shaken him considerably. He'd have to keep on reminding himself *never* to let the man know he was from Boston. If he did Andy was sure it would be all up with him.

"Whew," observed Sam Plummer, mopping his forehead with his bandana. "That was a close one, all right, but now we can take a turn around the deck. I'm on my own until dinner and, since this will be your last free moment for a long time, we'd better make the most of it."

Exploring the deck, Andy was properly awed by seeing the guns firsthand. He stared at the heavy carronades and long guns that pointed menacingly to seaward. Touching one gingerly, he wondered what it would be like to hear them in action against the enemy. He drew back his hand quickly at the thought.

"Folger," his campanion said presently, his voice hushed. "Here comes Captain Decatur in his barge. He went over to Boston this morning for last-minute instructions."

Eagerly, Andy peeped over the bulwark for a glimpse of the man who was in command of their ship. The captain's barge, smaller and more ornate than the launch that had brought them to the ship, was approaching rapidly. The man sitting in the stern was younger than Andy had anticipated, then he remembered what the gunner he had met that morning had told him.

"Yes," confirmed Plummer in reply to Andy's observation. "Captain Decatur's father was a full commodore. And I wouldn't be at all surprised if he became one himself someday. Our captain's stern, but he's fair, and he's a true fighter. They tell as how his family wanted him to enter the clergy, but instead he up and joined the Navy. Cap'n Decatur was on board the *United States* the day she was launched — the first real frigate built for the Navy. Then he served in the Indies against the French at the very same time his father was commanding another ship, the *Delaware*."

Andy could see the captain clearly as the barge drew alongside. He noted the man's high forehead, long nose, solid jaw, and the alert blue eyes that took in every detail of his ship as she was being made ready for duty. Captain Decatur was clad in dress uniform — a blue coat trimmed with yellow, square lapels, a stand-up collar, and yellow trim at the buttonholes. His yellow buttons, white breeches, and white waistcoat fairly glittered in the late afternoon sun. Thus dressed, Decatur made a colorful figure, but there was also something purposeful about him. For a reason he could not fathom immediately, Andy felt glad he would be serving under him.

"You called him *Captain* Decatur," he whispered. "Earlier, Gunner Ransom said he was a lieutenant."

Sam Plummer looked his disgust at Andy's ignorance, then shook his head resignedly. "Anyone in command of a ship is called captain, whether he's actually a full captain by rank or only a midshipman. And you'd better not make the mistake of calling him Lieutenant Decatur if ever you cross his path."

Later, after Sam left him to go below, Andy stood on deck looking toward the city where a few lamps were beginning to twinkle and glow. Lights were beginning to wink at him from those islands in Boston Harbor which were inhabited, had supply stations, or carried warning lights. He knew their names by heart, as did every Boston boy, and, closing his eyes, he ran rapidly down the list: Peddocks Island, Grape, Thompson, Lovell, Calf Island, Long Island, Spectacle, Deer Island, as well as the many smaller dabs of land that dotted the great harbor, including those two sets of shoals called The Graves and Roaring Bulls. Opening his eyes again, he could no longer see the wide mouth of the Charles River that divided East Boston and Charlestown from the city proper. Only the position of the lights ahead told him where they were.

Staring at the lights, he was reminded of something old Cony had once said to him. "None of us ever is satisfied for long, Andy. You take the counting-house clerk, lounging on the wharf, looking wistful out to sea. And then you take the sailor lad, leaning on a rail, eying the city and the shore, wishing he was on land. Neither of 'em has enough sense to know when he's well off. Of course, depending on how you look at it, the tar has a little the best of it. From time to time he can get ashore, while the clerk seldom gets a chance to go to sea.

"That's a funny thing for you, lad," the old printer had continued. "When they've been at sea for a long voyage, sailors just can't wait to set their feet on land. Maybe just to see if it's really like the way it looked from the water. Then, after they've been ashore for a little bit, they're itching to give their feet the feel of a deck again. There were lots of seafaring men in my family. Once the sea takes hold of a man, it seldom lets go."

A few minutes later, groping his way below in search of the crew's quarters, Andy stifled a yawn. It had been a full day and his head was still in a whirl. It had been a hard one, too, what with getting adjusted to new surroundings and meeting new shipmates, including the strange little cook. His shoulder ached where the cord of his seabag had rubbed the skin raw. It would feel wonderful to close his eyes in slumber. His mind on the peaceful sleep ahead, he almost bumped into Sam Plummer in the gloom of the tiny compartment they were to share.

"Tomorrow will be a busy day," the freckle-faced lad told him, smiling. "Better get every minute of sleep we can. Say, I forgot. This will be your first night in a hammock. Maybe I'd better give you a hand."

"I don't see why they make us live in such a little hole," muttered Andy irritably.

"Why, Folger," replied Sam, "that's all to the good. Even the rats have a hard time finding this out-of-the-way corner of the ship. Just imagine if the corsairs boarded us some day. They'd never find us down here. We'd be snug as bugs in a biscuit while they clapped the rest of the crew in irons or made 'em walk the plank."

As he talked, Sam's fingers worked busily, unlashing the upper hammock for the newcomer. Andy looked at his new bed dubiously. It appeared far less comfortable than his companion claimed, but maybe it was all in getting used to it. At any rate, he was so weary that he was ready to flop down anywhere.

"Here, let me give you a hand up," said the youth solicitously. "Just put your foot on that rung in the stanchion and up you go."

Tired though he was, Andy got a foothold and, with Plummer's help, went vaulting into his bed. He landed slightly off center. To his great surprise, the taut canvas flipped him over against the bulkhead, sending him to the deck with a crash.

"Why, that's a shame," his companion said kindly as Andy picked himself up. "But sometimes it takes a bit of practice to get the hang of it."

Andy tried a second time, then a third and fourth, only to lose to the tautly stretched hammock which had now become his adversary. On the last try, he actually gained the center of the canvas, only to lose his balance once again.

Sitting on the floor, battered and weary, Andy groaned aloud. "All right, just let me be. I'll spend the night down here."

Andy sat there wordlessly, chin sunk gloomily in his hands, too tired to even lie down. Suddenly he became conscious of voices on the other side of the bulkhead.

"Just imagine," someone was saying. "I was up in the rigging when Blossom passed by below, carrying some oatmeal to sick bay. He couldn't see me behind the mast so I roars out, 'You there, Petal! Get below to your scurvy galley afore I slice your topknot. We don't want the likes of you topside!' Cook stops like he's been stabbed, looking around wild-like to see who's talking to him, but he doesn't think to look up, even when I call him a second time. Finally he shakes his fist at the wind and goes steaming off, madder than a plucked rooster. Funny how he hates that name Petal so. I swear he would have thrown a cleaver if he'd seen me!"

Listening, Andy became aware of many things. He remembered the cook's face when he had called him Mr. Petal, the wild rush for the ladder afterwards. He recalled the long, roundabout tour of the ship with Sam as he sweated beneath the heavy seabag. Now, on a whim, he stepped around the bulkhead and looked into the crew's quarters.

His suspicions were confirmed quickly. All of the hammocks in the forecastle had a proper sag to them, a sag which allowed the occupant to curl up safely and in comfort. His own had been stretched taut as a drumhead. Sam Plummer had gone to great effort to rig his hammock so tightly that not even a fly could have landed upon it.

A moment later, spilling over with indignation, he made a dive for his tormentor, raining blows upon him. But Sam Plummer burst into laughter for, hampered by the tiny space and his own weariness, Andy's punches simply bounced off the mess boy's hunched-up shoulders. Furious at his own impotence, Andy redoubled his efforts as his companion roared with laughter.

At last Andy's arms dropped to his sides and, after glaring at Sam for a moment, his own face broke into a grin. It was impossible not to like the good-natured lad, despite the aches and pains he had suffered at his hands all day long. When Plummer finally stopped choking with laughter and held out his hand, Andy was more than glad to clasp it warmly.

"You're all right, Andy," chuckled the mess boy. "I didn't know how long you'd go without catching on to the hazing, but you're a good sport. Now, though, I think we'd better rig your hammock proper so you can catch a few winks. You look like you could use them."

CHAPTER VI

ANDY WAS asleep almost before he hit the hammock. It seemed only moments later that someone was pulling at his shoulder roughly, trying to shake him from his perch.

"Andy," Sam Plummer was saying, "hit the deck. I declare you're the soundest sleeper I've ever seen. I've been shaking you for ten minutes. Time to go topside."

When, a few minutes later, he reached the weather deck, Andy was startled to see stars still floating overhead. He was used to arising early, but this seemed to be the middle of the night. But the bustle of topside indicated that sailors were no respecters of the dawn.

The activity of that first morning on board ship was something Andy would remember always. More than ever before in his life, he felt like a fish out of water — literally like a landlubber at sea — as he watched the hands swarm up the rigging, tend the anchor, and scurry about the deck to the commands of the petty officers, most of which were unintelligible to him. Above these gutteral growlings he could hear the occasional sharper orders issued by the officers, but these too made little sense.

"A spanking breeze from the west this morning," muttered Sam Plummer. "The captain's going to take advantage of it. That noise you hear is the windlass as they heave in the anchor. It won't be long and we'll be underway for certain, bound for the Mediterranean and the Barbary States. Take a good look at Boston, Andy. It's the last you'll see of her for awhile."

Struck by the realization that Sam was voicing an important truth, Andy looked toward shore. Nearly all the lights had flickered out, but in the first pale glow from the east he could see faintly the buildings along the shore line.

Andy had a feeling of unreality. He felt like pinching himself in order to make sure he was actually standing on the deck of an American man-o-war, ready to sail for distant parts. Yesterday he had been a town boy, a printer's devil for the *Columbia News-Gazette*, surrounded by friends. Now he was part of a new world, separated sharply from everything he had ever known.

"Step lively, sonny," barked a seaman and Andy dodged swiftly to keep from being overrun by a gang of sailors running a line through a block near his feet. High above him he could hear the shrill cries of men in the rigging. The realization that he was a part of this orderly confusion under the morning stars set his blood to tingling. He, Andy Folger, was a tar on the *U.S.S. Enterprise!*

With a start, Andy realized they were moving. The ship was underway. He turned for one last look at Boston. Sam was right — it would be a long time before he would see the shores of the United States again.

The sun was up long before they had cleared the harbor. Almost at once Andy began to feel a slight twinge of uneasiness in his stomach. There was something about the roll of the sloop as they reached the open water of the Atlantic, something about the uneven tilt of the deck that made it difficult for him to stand. It was even more difficult for his stomach to catch up with the rest of his body.

"It's glorious to be at sea again, Andy" observed Sam Plummer as he joined his fellow cabin boy. "It's right fine visiting port and seeing the sights of land, but when you come right down to it, there's nothing like a rolling deck beneath your feet and all the Atlantic for a playground."

Andy clenched his teeth and tried to keep his balance as his friend rattled on. "Best of all, we've got plenty of provisions on board. Fresh milk, fresh fruit, and case after case of bully beef. I tell you, we'll eat royal this voyage."

Andy began to wish that Sam would change the subject, but his cheery companion continued, "Blossom tells me he's going to serve gobs of rice pudding soaked in thick cream for breakfast and a double helping of salt pork for lunch."

With difficulty, Andy wobbled to the rail. For one awful moment he was sure he was going to be sick. He managed to take a great gulp of the fresh salt air and felt slightly better. Reluctantly, on news that Blossom would like him to lend a hand in the galley, he made his way below. Will power alone helped him descend the ladder, but the strong smell of greasy food that assailed his nostrils before he reached the galley was too much for him. He took one more step, hesitated on the last rung of the ladder, then blurted, "See you later, Sam."

Hanging over the rail a few minutes later, Andy felt better but he knew he had made an unholy spectacle of himself.

He heard a laugh and a voice saying gleefully, "Well, mates, it looks as if they sent us the greenest landlubber in Massachusetts this time. Green in more ways than one! How they expect us to fight the corsairs with a mouse like this cluttering the deck is more than I can savvy. Though maybe he'd scare 'em off if they could see him the way he looks now. Ain't he a pretty sight?

This was followed by a roar of laughter from the others. Although Andy felt too ill and too humiliated to turn his head, he knew that the speaker must be the boatswain, the one they called Criter. He remembered that yesterday he had tripped over the big man's foot while toting his seabag during the long goose chase Sam had led him and how the husky tar had cursed and threatened him with the back of his hand the next time.

Tears stung his eyes. It was bad enough to be sick, but to be taunted about it at the same time was too much. Andy was wishing ardently that he could set foot on solid earth once more and never see the ocean again, when a hand fell on his shoulder and he recognized the voice of Gunner Ransom.

"Pay him no mind, lad," the gunner said quietly. "There's nothing to be ashamed of in feeling queasy to your stomach. There are few men on board this vessel who haven't had a touch of seasickness at some point in their sailing days. You think the world is coming to an end, then when you get your sea legs, you'll forget there ever was such a thing and go scampering about the deck as though you owned it. Now's the time to get it out of your system."

Andy felt weak as a kitten, but considerably better. He even managed a smile and a few words of thanks. Later, he succeeded in making his way below to the galley, ready to be instructed in his new duties by Blossom and Sam.

"First thing to remember," Blossom told him, "is to show up spick-and-span whenever you report for duty. I run a clean galley and that's the way I want my mess boys to be too. Clean hands, clean fingernails, clean uniform — and keep that way. Your job is to get food to the wardroom and mess hall quick, spilling as little as possible no matter what the weather. Sam will show you how to serve meals to the officers and how to go about the rest of your chores — washing dishes and helping me to keep this galley slick as a whistle.

"Feeding ninety-four men three meals a day is a big job," Blossom went on. "I haven't got time to tend to all the other details so you two have your work cut out for you. Also, you'll be given a place, port or starboard, and will stand your watches whenever they don't interfere with your duties down here. Meantime, you'll have to pick up all you can about a sailing ship, manning the guns and the rest of it, as best you can."

The cook paused to stir one of the kettles, then looked at Andy. "By the way, Sam tells me that you're from Boston."

Andy began to clear his throat nervously, but Blossom continued, "Boston, my favorite port. When my sailing days are done, that's the place I'm going to settle down. I'll find me a rocking chair and put my stocking feet in front of a roaring fire and sleep for two solid weeks without so much as frying a single gob of hen fruit."

Andy's open mouth betrayed his astonishment. Recovering, he darted an angry glance at his fellow mess boy. Sam's lips twitched at the corners, then spread into a grin that suffused his entire face, and Andy couldn't keep from smiling. Before they knew it, the two youths were rolling helplessly with laughter while the cook stared at them in wonder.

"Beats me," exclaimed the pudgy little man. "I didn't know 'Boston' was such a funny word, but I'm not complaining. They say a happy ship is a good ship. If that's so, this must be the best ship afloat."

By the third day at sea, Andy knew full well that there was a wide gulf between dangling one's legs from the wharf, watching a trim craft splash its anchor into Boston Bay, and actually serving on a man-o-war. Life on board was work and sweat and strain, with sleep available only when you could grab a few winks. By now, he was used to a hammock and dropped off to slumber almost before he hit the canvas. Yet it seemed that no sooner had he fallen asleep than someone was shaking him for his watch or duty in the galley. Officers on night watch usually wanted hot tea to keep themselves alert and Andy soon learned to find his way to the quarterdeck almost in his sleep, a pot of hot tea in hand. Happily, his seasickness had disappeared, just as Gunner Ransom had predicted, and before the week was up Andy was congratulating himself on having become an old salt.

This notion was a delusion, an easy trap, as he learned very soon, to his discomfiture. Every time he began to feel inclined to swagger across the deck, someone was sure to bring him down with a jolt.

"Avast there, lad!" Gunner Ransom would yell angrily. "Belay that whistling."

As Andy stopped in mid-air, the gunner would continue, "Don't you know that whistling is the captain's privilege only? Merchantman or man-o-war, the only man on board allowed to pucker up a tune is the captain when he's trying to whistle up a breeze."

Ransom would scratch the stubble on his chin, then add, "Seems it's about time I took you in hand and gave you a few glimmers about sailing. We can't send you back to Boston green as the day you come on board."

Squatting down, the gunner would take time to light the black stub of pipe, then cock an eye at his pupil. "We may as well begin at the beginning—with the timber itself," he said one day. "Building a ship is no easy matter. Much depends on the wood you have and how you use it. You take the timber itself, lad. Some of the best is American elm, English oak or plank, greenheart, mahogany, Quebec oak, and teak — usually each ship builder has his favorite. Curing the wood is as important as the wood itself. Unless your timber is seasoned right, you may not stay afloat long enough to dance a hornpipe.

"The best way to dry timber is to let the air get at it and season it natural-like. You got to stack it away from sun and wind, leaving an air passage between every piece on all sides. Let it stay that way, maybe three months to a year for soft woods and up to two years for harder woods. If you're going to season it with water, you dunk it in saltwater and let it stay there for a couple of years or more. Or you can take it out after a few weeks and stand it on end to dry.

"That should give you an idea, Andy," the man continued, "how hard it is to build a ship like the *Enterprise* — of all the work and care and planning that's gone into your home. And if you have anything to say about it, lad, never ship out on a vessel made of green timbers. Green wood is only half as strong as seasoned timber. You'd find out the difference soon enough."

The gunner tilted his face skyward and jerked a thumb at the great sails that billowed high above them. "Same with the sail. It takes a fine eye, skilled hand, and worlds of patience to turn out first-class sail. Without 'em, a ship could never leave its berth. And if they're poorly made or poorly cared for, you'll wish you'd never left the harbor. Because you're at the mercy of the sea when you leave the land behind — and that's a poor place to be with a rotten sail."

Guns told Andy a great deal more about the lore of sails. That night, down in the forecastle, Andy told Sam about the gunner's tutoring. "It's fair wonderful, Sam. I learned more about the *Enterprise* and sailing ships in one afternoon than in all the time I've been on board."

Sam pulled off one boot, then sighed wistfully. "You know, Andy, I've been at sea a lot longer than you and I never knew the half of what you've learned. I wonder if the gunner would let me listen in while he's going through his spiel."

"Of course he would," Andy said, impulsively. "I'm certain he'd be only too glad to have another pupil."

Sitting on the fantail next day, watching the gunner's blunt fingers fashion a lanyard for his guns, both Sam and Andy listened in awe as Ransom expounded his knowledge of the sea and the ships that sailed it.

"Some of this may not be new to you lads," the gunner began. "So stop me if you've heard it afore. But, speaking generally, you can never know too much about a ship, particularly your own vessel, and you never can tell when what you know will come in right handy. Take the different kinds of ships — such as your full-rigged vessel with its three masts. There you've got your foremast, main, and mizzen — all square-rigged. In a four-master, your after mast is known as the jigger-mast. In a five-master, you call the sails fore, main, middle, mizzen, and jigger, in that order, from stem to stern.

"A barque — that's a common type — has three masts with the fore and mainmast square rigged, while the mizzen is rigged fore and aft. Of course, a barque can have more than three masts but she's still a barque if all the masts except the first are square-rigged. A brig — that has two masts, both full square-rigged, while a brigantine is just the same, except she has no square mainsail.

"Now take your schooner — that has two, three, or even more masts, all rigged fore and aft — while a topsail schooner has a fore and aft foresail with a square fore-topsail."

The gunner paused for breath. "All this may sound like a lot of stuff and nonsense to you, but after you've trod the deck for many a year, you'll know it as easy as you'd know the color of your cap. So much for the different types of ships. Next, you've got to consider men-o-war. Ships of the line, they're the biggest critters afloat. The British dote on 'em, and let me tell you, lads, that it's a queasy feeling in the pit of your stomach to see one bearing down upon you. Nelson and Rodney have sent many a vessel to the bottom with their ships of the line.

"Generally," he went on, "they have two or maybe three gun decks and may carry anywhere from seventy-five up to one hundred and twenty-five guns on board. Compare that with the dozen guns we've got on the *Enterprise* and you'll see what I mean. Still and all, I'll stake our new American frigates against them any time. They were designed and built by Joshua Humphrey, the finest ship builder in the world, I says, and they'll stand up against anything. They've got only one gun deck, as compared with ships of the line, but they're speedier, have finer lines and stouter scantlings than any British frigate.

"They tell me that the *President*, one of the half-dozen frigates Humphrey has built since 1794, has a thicker side than the British ship of the line, *Hero*. Our frigates have first-class batteries, too, even though they don't stack up with the number carried by the larger British craft. Take our *Constitution*, for instance. She's listed as a 44-gun frigate, yet she really carries fifty-four."

Gunner Ransom paused to relight his pipe, then went on, "Next, you've got the sloop of war, or schooner, just like the *Enter-*

prise. As you see, our armament is mounted on the spar deck. Mostly we're used for scouting duty or for tackling enemy craft our size. Or, at least, we hope the other craft are our size."

Here Ransom broke off abruptly. "I've been driveling off at the mouth for hours, I'm sure," he said ruefully. "One of you must be due for a watch or down in the galley. I don't want to give you a permanent headache with all these facts, either."

After several sessions with the gunner about ships and sail, Andy realized more and more that he was far from an "old hand" on board. Ordered to dispose of the breakfast garbage one morning, he struggled up the ladder with the heavy slop bucket, only to find that he was once again in danger of being deathly sick. Adjusting himself to the roll of the ship, he made his way to the bulwark and, summoning all his strength, prepared to pitch its contents into the Atlantic. Unhappily, he failed to realize that the brisk breeze that had blown all morning had now become a stout wind. Also, he did not notice that the ship had taken a new tack and that he was no longer on the leeward side.

With one supreme effort, Andy flung the bucket upward and out, then jerked it to a halt. The garbage flew out, met the wind, and retreated before it. At least half found its way back to the deck. There was a sudden curse and Andy knew that a passerby had been liberally doused. His heart sank as he turned to view the victim — Bos'n Criter!

Even as Andy swung around, the boatswain's curses changed quickly to a roar of anger. For a second, the big man stood, dripping and sodden, his hair clotted with the remains of the oatmeal they had had for breakfast. Then, as a whoop of laughter from members of the crew who had seen the accident smote his ears, he sprang at Andy like a wounded bull.

Shaking with fright, the slender youth dropped the garbage bucket and stood paralyzed. Half-blinded by the oatmeal, the boatswain first snagged his foot on the pail, then slipped, and finally, with arms flailing wildly, went sprawling to the deck. There was another gale of laughter from the crew. Criter shot a murderous glance at the mess boy. "You did that on purpose," he bellowed. "Let me get my hands on you, Mouse. I'll slice you into such tiny bits there won't be enough left to feed the corsairs.!"

Clambering to his feet, Criter was starting toward Andy when a brusque command from the deck lieutenant brought him up short. "Boatswain! That's enough horseplay. Let the lad be. It was an honest mistake by a green hand and no great harm. Go below and clean yourself up."

Turning to the mess boy, the lieutenant said, "As for you, lad, I want you to swab this deck clean and then holystone it till the planks are fit to eat on. From now on, heave all trash over the lee side."

The officer's manner was severe, but Andy detected a small flicker of amusement behind his eyes. Andy had a suspicion the lieutenant had enjoyed the incident as much as the others.

However, the boy realized that he had not heard the last of the affair when later the boatswain in passing gave him a malice-filled look. "You'll pay for this, lad," he gritted between clenched teeth. "Nobody makes a fool of Rem Criter and goes scot-free to gloat over it."

Sam Plummer laughed merrily when Andy related the garbage-spilling incident, then lost his grin as he learned of the boatswain's threat.

"I doubt there's a man on board who wouldn't have given his eyeteeth to have seen what happened," said the freckle-faced lad. "Bos'n Criter is a loud-mouthed bully who vents his spleen on anyone half his size, but he's an ugly customer if he thinks you're making sport of him. I wouldn't go walking past him on a dark night, Andy, leastways not near the rail. There might be a splash and you'd be swimming in the Atlantic all alone."

CHAPTER VII

HAPPILY FOR Andy, there were others on board the *Enterprise* who more than made up for men like Criter. In addition to Sam, Blossom, and Gunner Ransom, the cabin boy found himself drawn to Jaime Rand, the young quartermaster. Casual and friendly, the easy-going Virginian had accepted Andy as a shipmate immediately, never making him feel like a despised landlubber. Often, as they stood night watch, Jaime at the wheel and Andy standing by as messenger, the Massachusetts lad found the hours slipping by very quickly as the quartermaster opened new worlds to him.

When Sam had told him that the Virginian had been to college and planned to become a history professor when his enlistment was up, Andy's admiration was even greater.

"Yep, Andy," Sam had said, "Jaime's a whizzer and no mistake about it. He knows as much about history as navigation and that's a lot. He made a cruise to China when he wasn't much older than you or me. When the quartermaster on board got sick, Jaime took over his duties and helped the captain navigate. This is his second cruise on board the *Enterprise*, so you can bet he knows heaps more now.

"They tell he turned down a commission because he doesn't intend to make the Navy a career, but if you ever notice, him and the captain get on first-rate. I've a hunch Captain Decatur likes him a whole lot, but of course he's not allowed to show it."

Now, standing mid-watch, the deck creaking beneath his feet and stars flickering overhead, Andy glanced sidewise at the young man at the ship's wheel, and wondered what it must be like to attend college — or, for that matter, to attend a school of any sort.

"A nice night, eh, Andy?" the quartermaster said presently. "As they say, if the moon be bright and clear when three days old, look for clear skies ahead. There's a lot to those old sayings," he went on. "Like a clear moon means frost; a single halo around it, look for a storm, or a new moon on her back brings wet weather. Landsmen are apt to scoff when they hear a sailing man predict the weather, but I'll go along with the old tars. Every now and then they may miss, but more times than not, they call the turn right on the barrel head. You can bet there's more to it than scuttlebutt when a saying has weathered the years."

Casting a practiced eye toward the heavens, Jaime gave a sigh. "The moon and stars mean a great deal to the sailing man, as you'll find out before you've spent many months at sea. Besides telling us where we are and tipping us off to the weather, the moon exerts a powerful influence on the sea. The sun is ever so much larger — maybe twenty-five or thirty million times as large — yet it's gravity pull is less than half that of the moon because the sun's so much farther away. We see gravity pull in action every day in the ocean tides. In fact, it's almost as though the water was being pulled out or drawn towards those planets. When you get the sun and moon pulling together on the same side of the earth, that's when you get the highest tides."

Andy scratched his head. "Jaime, I knew about the tides in

Boston Harbor, but no one ever told me why they happened and I never thought to ask. As I remember, though, they had high tide twice a day, not just once."

"That's true, Andy," replied the quartermaster. "You see, as the globe whirls about completely in a twenty-four-hour day, the tidal wave travels once around the earth. There are two high water marks because the tidal wave is double, so every ocean coast gets two high and two low tides every day. But the times change from day to day. As the moon goes revolving around us, it takes about fifty-four minutes longer to reach the same spot next day. So the tides show up later. We don't notice the tides out here in open water, even when the ocean may rise four feet.

"Where it really counts is when you're beating your way in or out of port and want to take advantage of the tides best suited to what you aim to do. It's important also when you're going to tie up alongside the quay. If you moor too taut on a high tide, you're apt to pull something loose, including pilings, when the water runs out from under you. On the other hand, if you're mooring on a low tide, you can't leave too much slack or you'll practically float away when high water comes in again. That's why we have to keep shifting lines when we're alongside a dock."

"I didn't know that anybody knew so much about anything," Andy said in some awe.

Jaime laughed good-naturedly. "Being able to sing out those few scraps of information is less wonderful than you may think, Andy. That's just a tiny portion of what every shipmaster must cram into his head. In addition to knowing his navigation forward and backward, he must know every spar and sail, every plank of his deck and keel, his cargo and how to store it, what to do in case of foul weather, how to handle privateers, and a thousand and one other things. And in the case of a man-o-war such as this, he's got to know his guns as well. Being captain of a ship may look like a prime job, but there's a heap more to it than wearing shiny buttons and giving orders to the hands. It's a lonely job and it takes a strong man to stand up under the responsibilities that go with it."

Later, groping his way down the dark passageway to the cramped quarters he shared with Sam, the cabin boy sighed disconsolately. There was so much to learn about the world, so much to discover about just this one ship! As he slid wearily into his hammock and closed his eyes for the few remaining hours of sleep before dawn, Andy wondered if he'd ever know one-tenth as much as Jaime Rand. At the moment, he'd be glad to settle for far less.

Navigation wasn't the only subject Andy knew little about, as he soon learned. True, he was beginning to get the feel of the deck beneath his feet and he hadn't spilled garbage on anyone since the Criter incident. But he was woefully lacking in other phases of seamanship, as he discovered when one of the tars conducted lessons in line and knots on the fantail. Almost before the instructor had begun, Andy blushed shamefully, aware that his capabilities in handling line were limited to lacing his boots or tying a bundle of the *Columbia News-Gazette*.

"Get this through your noggins once and for all," the deckhand was saying. "Rope is the most important thing we got on this here ship. Without it, the sails don't mean a thing and without the sails, our guns are worthless."

By now, Andy was beginning to realize that each man on board thought his own job and equipment the most vital items on the ship, but the boy wisely kept his silence.

"Good line is the key to the sea," the tar went on. "If you haven't got it, fail to take proper care of it, or don't know how to make use of it, you may as well rot in port because you don't belong at sea. It can easy mean the difference between living and dying, and before I'm through, every one of you will know your rope if I have to beat it into you with a monkey's fist."

Andy sweated to keep pace with the others but long before the seaman had finished his instructions, the cabin boy was lost hopelessly in a tangle that little resembled the knots they were supposed to tie. No doubt about it, he was all thumbs.

"Ropes are made of manila, hemp, or cotton," the sailor said, "and each plays an important part, whether you're on a man-o-war or merchantman. Hemp, now that's best for standing rigging or when you need a heavy purchase. Manila, we use that for running light rigging, while cotton comes in handy for man ropes, ridge ropes, and yoke items and lines.

"You make a rope by twisting yarns into strands and then laying 'em up spiral-like so that each yarn takes the strain evenly. As you see, the strength of a rope depends on the strength of each yarn. Unless you handle those yarns mighty careful, and twist 'em evenly, you've got a rope that's apt to part when you need it most. So you take your time to make sure the strands are even, smooth, and laid close.

"Too, you got to get the gather of how to lay a rope. A cable-laid rope — that's made up of three hauser-laid ropes, twisted contrarilike so that you really have a nine-strand rope. A shroud-laid rope is four strands, twisted in the direction of the sun. Then you take your hauser-laid rope — that's three strands of rope, laid right-handed going with the sun."

The deckhand paused long enough to spurt a stream of tobacco juice as Andy tried desperately to remember everything that had been told them.

"Now that you got a general idea of how ropes are made, the next thing to keep in mind is how to put them together and how to use them. Splicing, that's real important, as you'll find before you've spent a week at sea. There are two ways of putting ropes together — by knotting or splicing. When it comes to running rigging, you can see that splicing is the only answer because it's certain you can't jam an ugly knot through the sheave of a block.

"There are different ways of splicing, too. There's a short splice, long splice, eye splice, and a couple of other ways we won't go into right now. In the main, though, you take two ends of a rope that's been cut and start, just as I'm doing here, and unlay the strands a foot or so. Watch close and you'll see that I take the three strands of one rope in my left hand and one strand of the other rope in my right. Pass it over, tuck it through, and haul it taut. Do the same with the next strand and then with the third, just like this. Turn the rope around and do the same with the other end. There's your short splice, easy as apple pie."

Watching the tar's nimble fingers form the splice, Andy felt like a trout at a taffy pull and flushed as the sailor glanced his way.

"I'd say you need a little practice, sonny," remarked the tar dryly, "but keep your spirits up. Boston wasn't built in a day."

Down in the galley, as Andy snatched a spare moment to practice with a length of line, Blossom turned from his stove long enough to shoot him an inquiring glance. For a second, the mess boy was afraid he would draw a sharp reprimand, but the cook only grinned.

"So they're giving you the bitter end of the rope, eh, lad? From the way you're frizzling that line, I'd say you didn't know the difference between a square knot and a midshipman's hitch. Tell you what, Andy. After I've put these biscuits to bed and get the galley squared away, I'll lend you a hand. I've got a fair know-how when it comes to line and rigging, even though I've never let the deckhands get a whiff of it.

"They're a scurvy lot and if ever they found out I could roll a sheepshank with the best of 'em, they'd have me up the rigging night and day, with time off only to heat up vittles for their gullets. So the only condition I make is that you keep this between the two of us. If you've got five fingers on each hand, I guarantee we'll jostle the sweat out of that know-it-all deck gang or I'll start eating my own cooking."

True to his word, Blossom gave his time freely to help his young assistant learn the intricacies of line and knots.

"Practice is the big thing, Andy," the cook said. "For a time, you may feel that you'll never get the hang of it. But then, as in most other things, if you just keep plugging away, everything will fall into place one day and you'll have the hang of it so simple you'll think that you were born with a line in your hands.

"We'll start with the reef knot and then take the others one at a time. That's your most common knot, next to an overhand tie, because you always use it to tie the reef points of a sail. First, take your overhand knot, which you already know, then pass the ends, like this, so they take the same lay as the crossed parts of the overhand knot — and there you are. Unless you do it so, you'll wind up with a granny or lubber's knot.

"Next in handiness is the bowline, and you'd best never let a salt breeze spank your cheek without it. To form a bowline, hold the end of the rope in your right hand and take the standing part in your left. Lay the end over the standing part, turn the bight of the standing part over it so's it forms a loop with the end through. Lead the end around the standing part above the loop, bring it down, and you've got yourself a sure-enough bowline.

"From there, you can go on to make a bowline on a bight, running bowline, and all the others. But that's enough for one day. Once you get the hang of the reef and bowline, there'll be plenty of time to go on to the two half hitch, fishermen's bend, midshipman's hitch, and the rest. You'll find there's a time and place for every knot. You'll come to learn that rope is a sailor's best friend, next to a spanking fair breeze off the quarter."

CHAPTER VIII

ANDY'S FIRST intimation that something was wrong came when the ship took a long, heavy roll. A stool skidded across the galley, giving him a sharp crack on the shins.

Blossom gazed thoughtfully upward. "It seems awful quiet up there, but from the feel of that last one, the breeze must be freshening."

Hearing Cook's mutter as he rubbed the welt on his shin, the cabin boy recalled that the water had looked a bit queer when the duty last took him topside. He had been so absorbed in what he was doing that he had neglected to glance at the skies. He realized suddenly that no true seaman would have been found wanting in that way. The first act of any tar on popping from a hatch was to cast a weather eye aloft.

Andy was due on deck a little while later and took a careful look around him. The sea appeared unnaturally smooth, except for an infrequent oily swell like the one he had felt below. There was no breeze, contrary to Blossom's surmise. A stifling lack of wind made the mess boy gulp for air.

As he put the pot of tea he was carrying on a stand near the quarterdeck, Andy overheard the officer of the deck say, "I don't cotton to the looks of it. The glass continues to fall. If it keeps going in that direction, the quicksilver may run out altogether."

There was a scattering of clouds in the southeast, but otherwise the late afternoon sky was still a vibrant blue. As he gathered up cups and saucers, he was surprised to see Captain Decatur climbing the ladder to the quarterdeck, a foul-weather coat slung over his arm.

When Andy imparted this information to Blossom, the cook gave him a quizzical glance, then said casually, "Think I'll go topside and take a look myself."

When he returned, the cook's shoe-button eyes looked worried. "Let's secure all gear, lads. I want every pot and pan snugged down tight. It looks as though we're in for a bit of a blow. Nothing to get worked up about, though," he added. "The old *Enterprise* has made her way through wind and seas afore. We'll just sit tight and let 'er rip."

Andy was conscious of the cook's good-natured attempt to dispel his fears, but his words served only to whet the boy's curiosity about this, his first storm at sea. After they had snubbed down every movable article in the galley, he climbed the companionway again. The seas were still glassy smooth, but now there was an occasional puff of wind. He could hear the deck lieutenant bellowing to the hands, ordering them to batten down the hatches.

Even in his brief time on board, Andy had witnessed seas far worse then these, and it was difficult to understand the urgency with which the old hands moved about. He looked at the setting sun, now a glowing red ball in the west, then walked around the deckhouse, shaking his head in wonder. He glanced toward the southeast and stopped abruptly, sucking in his breath sharply.

The horizon in that direction was black with towering thunderheads that seemed to have no top. They were still some distance from the ship, but they moved swiftly, carrying the night with them. An occasional whitecap scudded toward them as the first fingers of the storm skipped over the water. Andy realized that the *Enterprise* was directly in the storm's path. It seemed to him that the sky was getting ready to topple down on them. His throat grew dry. Now he understood full well the urgent bustle of the crew and the grim expressions of the officers.

"Lad! Over here. Lend us a hand with these guns."

Andy turned to see Gunner Ransom kneeling on the deck with one of his gun crew, busily engaged in the process of securing a carronade.

"We're in for a squall, lad," Ransom said simply. "We'll need every pair of hands we can get, so fetch along with me. Benson, Andy here'll lend me a land. You go check on the aft batteries."

A feeling of relief surged through the boy. At a time such as this, it was far better to have something to do than to stand idly by, waiting for the storm to strike. He held thongs and line for the gunner as Ransom clogged the four wheels of the gun carriage and fastened the screw nut of the mooring chain.

Ransom looked up at the black thunderheads rolling toward them. "Dirty weather for sure, lad. You stick close to me when the seas get ugly. A man can go overboard in a whisk and there's precious little can be done to get him back."

Andy realized that he was beginning to be deathly afraid. He forced himself to look down, concentrating on the gun fastenings as the first drops of rain splattered against them. Although he knew what was coming, the boy was unprepared for the first terrific gust of wind that struck them a shattering blow.

The *Enterprise* heeled heavily. Andy, clinging to a deck cleat, was sure the ship would keep right on going over. Then, just as it seemed nothing could prevent it from turning turtle, the sloop halted its long roll and began, ever so slowly, to right itself. Now the boy fought desperately to keep from sliding across the deck in the other direction.

"That does us for a starter," yelled the gunner in his ear. "Take another turn on this cannon afore the next one hits."

Blackness closed over them, bringing fresh terror to Andy as the wind tore at the ship with mounting fervor. The lookouts had been ordered down from the crow's nests, but now shafts of lightning illuminated tiny figures silhouetted high above them, battling their way up the masts.

"Taking in canvas," shouted the gunner. "They'll furl the mainsail, then stow the mizzen topgallant and royals. Captain needs a bit of canvas to keep a head on her. But if he leaves too much up there, this gale will catch it and start popping masts like dry kindling."

Andy stared at the men aloft as they tugged to furl the topgallant.

One man edged his way out along the smooth spar, the multiton sail almost knocking him from his slippery perch. He nearly lost his grip as the spar tilted downward toward the angry sea, then he caught and held the pole with both arms. To Andy, it was inconceivable that anyone could be brave enough to go aloft, let alone make his way along a slithery spar that threatened to hurl him into the ocean at any second. Andy felt he could watch no longer. Hands locked around the cleat in the lee of the deckhouse, he shut his eyes and pressed his cheek tightly against the planking. When at last he gathered courage to look upward once more, he saw that the men aloft had succeeded in reefing the sail. Thankfully, he turned his attention to the bridge. Captain Decatur and the officer of the deck clung to the rail, heads lowered against the buffeting storm. A flash of lightning revealed two men lashed to the ship's wheel, fighting to quarter the seas. Andy knew that one of the men was Jaime Rand.

Limited though his knowledge was, he understood that it would be the last of the *Enterprise* if the ship were allowed to wallow in the trough of the heavy seas. Sam Plummer, whose turn it was to stand messenger duty this watch, must be on the bridge too. A sheet of rain shut the bridge from view and Andy breathed a little prayer that Sam was all right.

Slowly the ship began to climb, pointing its nose skyward as its bow was forced upward by a huge wave. Up it went until, reaching the crest, it hung there suspended for a brief, terrible second, then began its descent. As it did so Andy felt as though they were dropping into a bottomless pit.

The ship's long fall was halted by a sickening blow as the bow struck solidly, shivering the *Enterprise* from stem to stern and sending the black water cascading over them. Soaked to the skin, Andy was sure that everyone on the bridge must have been washed overboard by the force of the wave that had hit them. It seemed impossible that the *Enterprise* itself could still be afloat. To his great surprise, the next angry flash of lightning revealed the men still on the bridge.

The battering from the giant storm was unceasing, without respite. Andy ached from the blows that the unending roll of the vessel dealt him. First he was slammed against the deckhouse as the ship tilted to starboard. His arms seemed to be yanked from their sockets as the long roll to portside began. Andy had time to wonder how Billy Blossom was faring below. He hoped the little cook was not foundering in a sea of pots and pans. Just then a great surge of water shivered the ship and he felt his hands being wrenched from the cleat.

Andy went sliding across the deck until he banged into the port bulwark. He lay helplessly as the ship began its slow return roll to starboard. Again he began to slide, this time more swiftly, at an angle that would carry him past the deckhouse. There was no bulwark in his path on the starboard side, only guy lines and open water. He was sliding directly toward the gap in the ship's side when a strong arm caught him in a grip of iron. Slowly the arm drew him to the shelter of the deckhouse.

Gunner Ransom's voice sounded in his ear. "Easy, laddie. Petal Blossom would never forgive us if we let his mess boy go over the side."

Blinded by rain and salt spray, Andy clung thankfully to the cleat once more, partly protected by the bulky figure of the gunner. But now there was a new danger. Ransom was shouting, "One of the guns working free — screw nut loose. Hold fast. If it gets away, you try to stay clear — "

Andy suddenly remembered that he had heard a tar tell of a carronade that had broken away on another vessel. Roaring about like an uncontrolled monster, it had killed four men, maimed a score of others, and smashed a deckhouse before it had been captured.

Now, through the howling winds, he heard the creak of the gun chain as the screw nut worked free under the roll of the sea. If the heavy carronade broke loose, nothing would impede its journey. In a storm such as this, it would be an instrument of certain death to anyone in its path. There was a flash of lightning and Andy saw something else — an extra length of short chain wrapped around two hooks on the deckhouse bulkhead. One hand clinging to the cleat, Andy's other hand grasped the chain and unwound it. He began to crawl up the deck toward the gun. Gunner Ransom must be somewhere up ahead in the blackness.

A long, powerful roll almost did for him, but his nails bit into the slippery deck and he somehow managed to keep from sliding. Then he felt the bulkhead. The groaning of the sloop's timbers was terrifying in a sudden lull from the storm's roar. With great difficulty, Andy worked his way along the bulkhead, dragging the length of chain. Now he could make out the dim figure of the gunner and, beyond him, the ominous outline of the heavy carronade. Ransom turned his head and Andy could see the astonishment in his eyes as the boy crawled toward him.

Even as he moved forward, the screw nut pulled free with a sickening shriek and the heavy carronade began to move of its own volition. The iron monster slid a few inches, then, as the ship rolled in the opposite direction, crashed back into the bulwark.

They would have no second chance. Now heedless of the storm, man and boy somehow got the carronade back into place. Gunner Ransom slipped a wedge between its wheels, chocking the gun with a piece of chain. Andy's chain was already around one wheel, secured to a chock. The *Enterprise* began another giant roll. They held their breaths as the gun strained against its fetters. It held. Together, they managed to snub it more securely with extra lengths of line and chain. They waited long enough to make certain it was firmly bound, then made their way laboriously toward the deckhouse. Utterly spent, Andy had to be dragged the last few feet by the gunner.

"The storm is easing, lad," breathed Ransom at last. "We've

a long way to go, but the *Enterprise* is still afloat and the worst is over."

Andy tried to reply, but no words would come. Relief flooded over him.

CHAPTER IX

"SAM! ANDY! You lads get below to the galley on the double," snapped Billy Blossom. "I want a word with you two."

Andy shot his companion a questioning glance as they fell in step behind the cook, but the towheaded mess boy shrugged his shoulders and whispered, "I don't know what it's all about, but he's mad for fair."

Blossom slammed the galley door shut behind them and began to pace his tiny domain in furious silence. Finally, he turned to glare at the two boys. "Well, it looks as though you're in the soup now. Though, at the moment, I don't know which of you is guilty."

A pudgy finger jabbed at them menacingly, "Another batch of crullers is missing! I discovered it when I came below to open up this morning. One of you two lads is a sneak thief!"

Andy looked at Blossom in amazement as the cook continued furiously, "When that first batch was missing I thought maybe I'd just made a mistake and dreamt I'd made doughnuts — even though I caught the devil from the officers after I'd promised them fresh crullers. The second time I knew it was no mistake but that someone had broken in here and stolen the lot of 'em. Or sneaked in here."

Blossom's voice rose. "They told me it couldn't be anyone but one of my mess boys. At first I argued it simply wasn't so. Told 'em that I'd be willing to bet neither one of you had anything to do with it. Fact is, I felt I'd been square with you boys. I trusted you as I would've my own sons if I'd had any. I'd have bet my wooden teeth it couldn't have been either of you. That's why I refused to make you two turn in your keys to the galley."

The little man was hot with indignation, but his anger now seemed tinged with sorrow as he said more calmly, "Now they've got a case against you and no mistake. One of the deck force saw someone sneaking out of here last night with a bundle hidden in his blouse. He swears it was one of you tads, but you were too quick for him to tell who it was." Blossom paused. "Now the only question is, which one?"

Andy stared at Sam. Surely the freckled-faced lad was too open-handed ever to pull such a trick. Then, to his horror, he realized that Sam was eying him sorrowfully, a half-formed question in his eyes.

Blossom gazed at them sadly and his voice dropped to a normal pitch. "That's all for now. I've no positive proof of which one did it, but I've no fear you'll give yourself away. And let me warn you, the officers and hands are in an angry mood. Most anything may go on land, but at sea, in the tight confines of a ship, the sneak thief gets short shrift. The mood they're in, the guilty party is liable to be drawn and quartered or thrown into the brig to live on stale biscuit and water until he's mustered out. Now I'll thank you both to hand back your keys to the galley. So far as I'm concerned, I want no conversation from either of you as you go about your duties."

Topside, walking slowly toward the fantail, Andy felt sick at heart. He was certain that Sam hadn't taken the crullers. Yet, if he hadn't, who had? Actually, the finger of suspicion must point at Andy as the newcomer. He was the likely suspect. Even though Blossom hadn't spelled it out, he seemed to think Andy had done it rather than Sam. He was innocent, but how would he ever convince the others of the fact? Shuffling along, racking his brain for some means of finding out who had done the pilfering, he was conscious of dark looks from the deckhands.

Stealing at sea was no small matter, even if the theft was of only the smallest of things. Evidently, someone had spread the word that Andy was guilty. Averting his eyes, he walked past a group of men as quickly as he could, then spied Gunner Ransom kneeling on the deck, tinkering with one of the cannon. The gunner started to speak, but instead turned his head and returned to his chore. Andy stood still for a fleeting instant, then, sick at heart, made his way to his quarters. To his surprise, Jaime Rand was waiting for him. "You say you didn't take the crullers?" Jaime asked at once.

"No siree!" replied Andy hotly. "I wouldn't! Not for all the tea in Boston Harbor. I had nothing to do with it. Trouble is, no one is going to believe me. It's easy to tell what everybody's thinking. Sam's been on board a long spell and nothing like this ever happened. I'm the newcomer. I'm the one they think took 'em."

The mess boy's face flushed and he added quickly, "Not that I think Sam had anything to do with it. He's too square for that. Sam isn't the sort."

"How could anyone gain entrance to the galley without a key? Is it an easy matter?"

"Not that I can see," answered the mess boy. "That's what makes it all the worse. Cook buttons up tight when he's through for the evening and fixes the top of the half-door with a hook. I'm afraid the only way it could be opened is with the key. And the only ones who had them were Sam, myself, Blossom, and the captain. I don't fancy Captain Decatur taking the crullers when he can have all he wants just for the asking. And it's certain that Blossom isn't hungry enough to down his own doughnuts. That leaves just Sam and me. I'd wager my life it wasn't Sam and that's for sure."

He paused uncertainly. "I didn't take them. Or, at least, I don't remember it if I did. But I'm so mixed up now that I'm half-ready to *say* I did."

The quartermaster stroked his chin meditatively. "Maybe it would be worth my while to have a little chat with Petal Blossom pretty soon."

Three days later, when Andy reported for duty in the galley he was surprised to hear Blossom whistling. Billy threw him a toothy smile as he dodged about among his pots and pans, readying dinner for the crew. Andy was astonished at the cook's good humor.

Presently Blossom halted before the boy. "You mean you haven't heard? Andy, my boy, this is just about the finest news I've had since reporting on board the *Enterprise*. I've done you and Sam a real disservice. But you have my word that I'll make it up to you."

Seeing Andy's bewilderment, the cook went on cheerily, "We've found our thief, lad. We've nabbed the tar who filched the crullers. Or at least we know who did the mischief, even if he's not been thrown in the brig yet. Bos'n Criter. That's your man."

Andy gaped in amazement. "Bos'n Criter? Are you sure?"

The cook winked at his mess boy. "No doubt about it, lad. He was tripped up plain and simple by a little plan suggested by Jaime Rand. The idea was so simple I wonder I didn't think of it myself. Jaime says, 'Cook, why don't you give the thief a taste of red pepper in his crullers or a little touch of castor oil? Or maybe a dash of both to whet his appetite?' "

Blossom chuckled. "I did just that, although I made Jaime swear he wouldn't let on what we were up to. You see, I was still halfway afraid you'd been pilfering and so I couldn't allow any sort of warning. I baked a batch of the finest crullers you ever did see and set 'em out to cool where most everybody on board could smell them and weep because they wouldn't be getting any. Only this time the crullers had red pepper and castor oil buried deep inside 'em. Last night I left the crullers sitting on my stove when I closed the galley tight as a drum. They were gone this morning, just as Jaime and I had figgered. So we sat back and waited."

The cook gave a triumphant snort. "We didn't have long to wait, either. Before the morning was half over, there was the most awful sneezing and caterwauling you ever heard down in the forecastle. Bos'n Criter had sneaked down there to taste one of the crullers he'd pinched. He must have jammed the whole doughnut into his mouth afore he noticed anything was wrong. I tell you, Andy, I didn't stint on the pepper or castor oil. Whoever took a bite would know it! The boatswain took off, bawling so fierce you could hear him from stem to stern. He must have downed a gallon or two of water, though it did him precious little good. The jig was up by then. We found the rest of the crullers stashed in his sea chest. Andy, I wish you could have heard Criter wail. Sounded as though he'd been run through with a saber."

Blossom chuckled, then added soberly, "And to think I'd almost given in to the notion that you or Sam had done it. I was relieved as well as pleased to hear the boatswain holler."

"Did you ever find out how Criter managed to get inside the galley?" asked Andy.

"Yep. He confessed to the whole affair when he saw there was no use playing innocent. Breaking into the galley was easier than any of us suspected. You know that tiny sliver of space near the bottom of the half-door? Well, Criter just took a strand of wire, slipped it in the opening, and worked it around to the hook. Then he led the wire to the side of the door and used the door as a brace to pull the hook open. After pinching the crullers, he closed it the same way, though that took a bit of doing."

Blossom shook his head. "I've learned my lesson. I'm having the carpenter yank out the hooks and replace them with a stout bolt. Though after the boatswain's experience, I doubt if we'll be troubled on that score for a long time."

Thinking of the talk about being drawn and quartered when he was a prime suspect, Andy asked nervously, "What will happen? What will they do to him?"

"Not a blessed thing, lad," the cook replied. "For one, he's needed too badly on deck to spend the rest of his life in the brig. When the captain heard about it, he only smiled and said he thought that a mouthful of red pepper was punishment enough. But you can just bet that Captain Decatur won't forget the matter when it's time for liberty, leave, or any special privileges for Criter. And you can wager Criter won't forget the matter, either. He still holds a grudge against you for spilling that garbage on him. Now he'll think you had a hand with Jaime Rand in tripping him up this time. I know it doesn't make sense, but that's the kind of brute he is. So make a point to keep out of his way, Andy, whenever possible. But if ever he lays a hand on you or Sam, I vow he'll regret it. I'll part his hair with one of these cleavers afore he knows what hit him."

"Land ahoy!" The hoarse cry from the forward crow's nest came drifting through the open hatch and brought an abrupt end to the conversation.

"Aye," Billy Blossom exclaimed. "That'll be Gibraltar somewheres off our port bow. I figgered we were about due to make a landfall. Once we get past the Big Rock, we're in enemy waters and no mistake."

The cook grinned at Andy. "Here's some slop that needs dumping. You better head topside and take a look for yourself."

On deck, Andy could make out what seemed to be an island rising dimly from the edge of the horizon. As the green water pushed its way past the bow of the *Enterprise*, he experienced a thrill of anticipation tinged with foreboding. It would be wonderful to see land again but, as Cook had pointed out, they would be in enemy waters once the sloop slipped into the Mediterranean —just that much closer to the dreaded Tripolitans.

What was the Greek legend that Jaime had once told him about this spot? That Hercules had opened the passage between Tangiers and Gibraltar, making it wide enough for sailing ships, yet narrow enough to prevent whales swimming through from the Atlantic. It was said Hercules had thrown up hills on either side to mark the straits for navigators. Jaime had said that many still called them the "Hercules Columns." Now at last, he, Andy Folger, was seeing them for himself.

As the day wore on and Gibralter became clearly visible as they drew nearer, Andy acknowledged the growing knot of fear he felt in his chest. At one moment, closing his eyes, he hoped that when he opened them again he would see Boston instead of an outpost of the Mediterranean. Working as a printer's devil on a Boston newspaper would be far preferable to being skewered on a Tripolitan blade — or, worse still, being captured and carried as a prisoner to the Pasha. Andy shuddered with misgivings. Then there was a joyous whoop in his ear and Sam was standing at his elbow.

"There she be," exulted the boy. "Good old Gibraltar, just as I left her, sitting in the sunshine, waiting to wink at us. I tell you, Andy, this has been a spanking rough trip on the everlasting Atlantic. Now maybe we can take us a breather on this little old pond."

Andy flashed a worried look at his happy-go-lucky friend. "Tell me, Sam, will we see any pirate craft today?"

At this the freckled-faced lad roared with laughter. "You're still green, my boy. Nope, it isn't likely we'll see any corsairs today or tomorrow or for many months. No one would be more surprised than me or Cap'n Decatur if we did. Unless it would be the corsair captain. It was just a manner of speaking when I called the Mediterranean a pond. It's a huge body of water, stretching all the way from here down past Alexandria in Egypt, with the fortress of Tripoli nearly halfway down the African coast. Nope, the Med is big enough to hide several squadrons our size without anyone knowing the difference.

"Mostly, pirates have smaller craft than ours, able to duck into shallow water where our big vessels can't go," Sam went on. "If one of our frigates caught up with a Tripolitan cruiser in open water, there wouldn't be enough left for Billy Blossom to serve for breakfast. Of course, an unarmed merchantman is no match for the corsairs, but they don't rove the seas so free and bold when they know an American frigate may be over the horizon."

The cabin boy's voice lost some of its exuberance. "Same time, their ships are big enough to give us a tussle. If we meet up with one, it would be a pretty even match, with the winner depending on guns, ship handling, and luck."

Sam gave a chuckle. "Anyway, I'd be willing to bet you my best boots we finish this cruise without ever getting within cannon range of the enemy. That's the way it was my last cruise. I'll wager it will be the same this time, even though they say Commodore Preble intends to carry the war direct to Tripoli."

CHAPTER X

THREE MONTHS later, Andy was to recall his friend's remarks as they sailed through the Straits of Gibraltar. The long cruise had lacked excitement. In all this time they had sighted just two enemy gunboats. When they were spotted, the corsairs hoisted full sail, kept their range, and lost the *Enterprise* under cover of darkness.

Sam had been right. Naval warfare was not as he had supposed it to be when, so long ago, he had dangled his feet on the edge of a Boston wharf. Battles were not fought every day, especially with an enemy as wary as this one. However, when they did go into action, he supposed it would be with a sudden fury. No one would then be sure he would see his native land again. Deep down, Andy was relieved that they had not been able to get within hailing distance of the enemy, although he would never have admitted this to the others. He had enough to keep him busy, serving meals to the officers and crew, working in the galley, standing the endless watches, and keeping out of Bos'n Criter's way. Twice Criter had nearly trapped him alone, but the boy had managed to give him the slip and to make it to the safety of the galley.

Now, dressing in darkness, getting ready to stand mid-watch,

Andy yawned, musing once more on the boredom of blockade duty. He knew that their main purpose was to protect merchantmen in the area, be they French, British, or of any other nation. According to Gunner Ransom, the time was not ripe for the *Enterprise* to attempt any assault on the fortress of Tripoli. And if that time did arrive, it was doubtful if the lightly armed schooner would be assigned much of a role in combat. Yet their very presence served as a reminder to pirate craft that a U.S. man-o-war was on patrol.

Climbing to the bridge, the boy brushed past the darkened figure of the helmsman, bundled against the cool night breeze. "Hallo," he said in surprise. "Where's Jaime? Didn't they call him for watch?"

"They called him all right," grunted the seaman, hunching over the wheel. "He's down with the fever and so they rolled me out. Believe me, if this sickness keeps up, we're going to be shorthanded all right."

Andy accepted this soberings news with a frown. Yesterday morning one or two deck hands had complained of aches and pains. When it became apparent they had a real fever, they had been sent below. The ship's doctor had made a quick check, but even before he had completed his diagnosis another tar collapsed on deck. Later, two officers were stricken and had to be assisted to their compartments. No doubt about it, some strange malady had overtaken the vessel.

"Doctor says he can't tell just what it is," Blossom had replied in answer to a question from the boy. "Only he hopes it isn't fatal. Some hands say it's food poisoning, but I figger it's something else. Who knows? Maybe it's something carried by an offshore breeze or maybe it's from some vermin we picked up when we took on supplies at Malta. I'd just as soon it was food poisoning, 'cause then they'd get it out of their systems in a hurry. But when fever strikes a ship, with everybody living so close and all, that's not good. And if I know Captain Decatur, he'll be heading for the open sea afore long. It's no time to be looking for trouble when the fever weakens your crew."

Now, glancing about in the darkness, Andy saw two or three new faces on the watch, as well as that of Lieutenant Higgins who was supposed to have had the last watch. Jaime was not the only tar, evidently, who had been felled during the night. Edging closer to Higgins, he could hear him speaking in a low voice to a midshipman who had just arrived topside.

"Aye," Lieutenant Higgins said. "It's not a good sign. By now, I venture half the crew is down with the fever. Bones can't do much about it but pop a pink pill into their mouths, give 'em a swig of sassafras juice, and let the fever run its course. Fact is, when the captain gave me the new course, he didn't look so good around the eyes himself."

Turning toward the compass, Andy felt a fresh breeze on his cheek and realized that Billy Blossom's prediction had come true. The *Enterprise* was making for open water. The officer dropped his voice, but Andy pricked up his ears as he caught snatches of the conversation.

"Bottomly gave out about six bells," Lieutenant Higgins continued. "We buried him during my watch. My first watch, that is. Wrapped a shroud around him and slipped him over the side. Couldn't take any chances holding services for him."

The remainder of the conversation was lost to Andy, but he was frightened by what he had overheard. Bottomly had been one of the first deckhands to drop the previous day. Now he was dead and gone. The dark seas into which the tar had gone so recently made Andy shiver. He recalled what old Cony had once told him about the ways of the sea.

"Ship to sea long enough," Cony had said, "and you'll become its victim. If the pirates or sickness don't get you, the sea will. Life at sea is enticing, with the waves dancing and smiling, waving you on, promising you adventure, riches or glory, but once it's got you in its clutches, there's little or no escape. Make one mistake and you're a goner. Sometimes you don't even have to make that mistake. Because the sea — it's always waiting and it's got worlds of time."

Staring aft into the blackness, Andy was struck by the realization that, but for the grace of God, it might well have been his body they had slipped over the side. Would he ever see the skyline of Boston again? With an effort, he turned his face forward once more.

"Lookee there," Lieutenant Higgins suddenly snapped as a light showed at a forward hatch. "Douse that glimmer." But there was no responding motion to obey.

Turning to Andy, the lieutenant growled, "Go forward, messenger, and put out that glim immediately. We're traveling dark tonight. I want that light out even if it's Bones himself."

Dawn broke gray and damp. Although Andy was heartened to see the first cheerless streaks of daylight, he was dismayed to discover that less than half the crew was on deck to man the brooms for morning sweepdown. If he was any judge, about two-thirds of the hands were missing. When he had been relieved as messenger and had made his way to the galley, he found Blossom even more glum than he'd been the previous evening.

"Sam Plummer is the latest to come down," he announced. "He

was working, pert as you please, when suddenly he slumps over and they tote him off to his hammock."

Blossom tugged at his ear, a sure sign that he was truly worried. "Bottomly was the first, but I'm afraid he's not the last. Once the fever takes hold, it sweeps a ship. Those who miss it can thank their lucky stars. Who can say how they do, either? Something in the blood keeps the fever out, or a tar's bile is too strong or something."

Blossom tried to grin. "Anyway, Andy, the two of us are whole and hearty and we'll give 'em merry Ned until we drop. Liquid's the only thing to keep fever away, so we'll keep tea and broth a-coming. You're going to have your hands full, lad. With Sam down, it's up to you to serve the wardroom and such crew as is on their feet."

Blossom hesitated. "I'm afraid you'll have to serve the others too, Andy. I don't like to ask you to do it but there's no help for it. The sick must be served. Those of us who are still able must tend their needs. I'll have you relieved from watch and other duties while you run vittles and drink below. Mind, though, have as little to do with the fevered hands as possible. Try to keep from touching anybody and, if you can prevent it, don't let 'em breathe on you. It'll be hard, but remember I need you on your feet."

Andy soon learned that Blossom spoke truth. Duty that day consisted of a series of round trips to the forecastle and officers' quarters, toting broth, hot tea, or water. He began briskly enough, but before mid-morning his visits below had become one confused blur. Despite Cook's warning, it became impossible not to come in contact with the sick, not to support a head or hold an arm as he helped a feverish seaman sip a mouthful of water or soup. Vaguely, he realized that one tar — or was it two? — had disappeared from his hammock since first he'd served him.

Jaime Rand and Sam Plummer were both alive. Jaime's pale forehead was burning hot, but the quartermaster feebly pushed away his hand when Andy attempted to cool it with a damp rag.

"No, lad," the Virginian whispered. "Keep your distance. Steer clear."

Sam Plummer was too weak to resist when Andy held his head and put a spoonful of broth between his parched lips. Andy realized that this was one of the few times he had not seen a smile on Sam's face. He lowered his partner's head gently to the hammock, but he could not tarry. Too many others were waiting. The sun broke through the clouds as the day wore on, but it lifted no one's spirits, least of all Andy's. Climbing ladders and making his way through hatches became a nightmare, while the heavy atmosphere of sickness that engulfed him every time he stepped into the forecastle sent waves of nausea flooding over him. Except for the fresh air, topside was little better. It became a grim struggle to make his way to and from the galley, carrying tureens, pitchers, and mugs. It was hard for his weary legs to function against the roll of the ship, and he had to fight hard to keep from dropping or spilling what he carried.

It was afternoon when the cry of "Sail ho!" rang out from the crow's nest. Everyone topside stopped in his tracks and gazed anxiously aloft.

"Sail on the larboard quarter," the look-out called. All heads swung in that direction. From the deck nothing could be seen as yet. Every man was silent, holding his breath.

Gunner Ransom suddenly appeared beside the cabin boy. "We're in luck if it's one of ours," he said softly. "They're sure to have a doctor on board to lend Bones a hand and a good medical chest, plus fresh water and provisions." Then a frown clouded the gunner's leathery features, "If it's not — well, if it's not one of our lads, that's not so good. We've not enough able hands to man two cannon, let alone anyone to climb the rigging or handle sail."

The officer of the deck aimed his trumpet at them. "Lad, you there. Stow your gear and report to the bridge for messenger duty. On the double now."

Gaining the bridge, Andy was not surprised to find that Lieutenant Higgins still held the deck. Unshaven, with red-rimmed, sleepless eyes, the man looked unbelievably weary. However, his voice was cool and casual. "Stand close by, lad," he ordered. "I may need two swift feet to run messages beyond my trumpet's range."

Tilting his face to the crow's nest, he put the trumpet to his lips. "Can you make her out?" he called.

"Hull coming into view, sir," came the reply and the officer reached for the long glass Andy was holding.

At that instant Captain Decatur appeared on the ladder. He climbed laboriously toward the bridge, assisted by a midshipman. Lieutenant Higgins lowered the glass and shot a startled glance at the fevered captain. For a second it appeared as though he were about to urge his commanding officer to return to his bunk, but instead he saluted sharply.

"Ship just over the horizon, sir. Forward crow's nest spotted her, but she's still hull-down from here."

Swinging the glass to his eye once more, the lieutenant gazed seaward, then muttered in supressed excitement, "I've got her now. Tripolitan cruiser! She'll go larger than us, I'm afraid, sir."

"Very well," replied Captain Decatur calmly. "Have they seen us yet, do you think?"

"If they haven't, they soon will on their present course," answered the officer grimly. "I'd wager they go eighteen guns against our dozen — if we had the hands to man that many. Shall I give the order to swing about? Though it may be difficult to evade them, what with the shape we're in."

"We can't outrun them," Decatur answered with finality. "We're no match for their speed."

He studied the dark speck, now plainly visible on the horizon. Just then a shaft of sunlight pierced the gray skies, illuminating the bridge. The commander's face brightened. "No, we can't outrun them," he said slowly, "but maybe we can try to catch them."

Lieutenant Higgins nearly dropped the glass in surprise. His voice was dubious as he asked, "Are you sure you're feeling fit, sir?"

Captain Decatur became more erect and there was the hint of a twinkle in his gray eyes. "Yes, Higgins, never fear. The fever hasn't affected my brain. I said we'd *try* to catch them, but I have a feeling we won't succeed. Somehow, if we can manage it, they're going to remain just beyond our reach and will eventually elude us. Now, I want every man-jack topside who can stand, lean, or sit."

As Lieutenant Higgins stared at him, the captain said grimly, "It's not going to be easy for the hands, but I imagine they'd rather die in the sunshine than be skewered in their hammocks. Give each man one or more weapons — swords, knives, pikes — whatever they can hold. When the time arrives, have them brandish the weapons aloft as though eager to see a corsair on the other end."

Suddenly he grinned at the brightening skies. "I imagine the gleam of our weapons will capture the sunlight almost as well as a mirror. What the enemy doesn't know won't hurt them."

"It might just work, Captain. Aye, aye, sir." Higgins' voice had taken on a new note of eagerness.

Slowly, in groups of two's and three's, including many who had to be carried, the ship's crew made its way topside. Those who were able took their places along the rail on the starboard side, others were propped against bulkheads or bales of rope. The very sick simply sat on deck, awaiting the command to wave weapons aloft.

"Keep her head slightly off course so the pirates can see only the starboard side," Captain Decatur commanded. "This may prove a bit ticklish. I want to give every impression of being eager to exchange broadsides, but we don't want to look so bad at ship-handling that her captain concludes we're landlubbers and displays the same confidence in attacking us."

Managing a forlorn smile, he added, "On the other hand, I certainly don't want to catch her."

Andy watched intently as the enemy vessel continued to close on a course that would bring it directly across the bow of the *Enterprise*. Lean, low, and black-hulled, the cruiser looked like a rugged adversary. It was Andy's first real glimpse of the enemy and it affected him deeply. It was difficult to comprehend that the decks of the oncoming vessel were swarming with corsairs seeking to destroy them. And, he thought, in honesty, every man on board the *Enterprise* was in these waters for the very same purpose — to defeat and sink the enemy.

"Every tar that's able and not needed on deck, scramble aloft," bellowed Lieutenant Higgins. "Make a show of activity as though we've just spied them and are trying to lay on canvas. Brandish your weapons every now and then."

Tension mounted as the enemy continued to hold course.

Andy found it difficult to swallow. He had to fight back an urge to break from the bridge to take refuge below. It was quite possible that Captain Decatur had guessed wrong and that the corsairs would be anxious to open the engagement. Then, when Andy was beginning to feel he could stand the waiting no longer, the Tripolitan cruiser broke course and began to veer swiftly toward the east, apparently seeking the shelter of a distant cloud bank.

The sigh of relief that went up from the crew was audible throughout the ship. Captain Decatur sagged noticeably, but there was a satisfied smile in his eyes. He waited a moment longer, then nodded to Higgins.

"Here, lad," ordered the lieutenant. "Help the captain below."

The comanding officer made no resistance this time. With Andy supporting him on one side and the aide assisting him on the other, they made their way below to his quarters, where Captain Decatur gasped his thanks as they helped him into his bunk.

Later, after the enemy vessel had disappeared into the distance, Andy expressed his feelings to Blossom. Standing among his pots and pans, Billy Blossom dabbed beads of perspiration from his forehead as he observed, "I won't go so far as to say that any man on board is eager to die in battle, but it's one thing to go down fighting and another to perish without a prayer or strength enough to swing a saber. Now, let's get busy getting the crew shipshape again."

CHAPTER XI

RECOVERED FROM the mysterious fever that had almost ended the cruise of the *Enterprise*, Jaime Rand lounged on deck with his friend Andy, soaking in the warm sunshine.

"Mediterranean — the middle-of-the-earth sea," Jaime said presently. "You know, Andy, this voyage seems momentous to us. Listening to the crew, one might be led to believe that all the nations of Europe and Africa had their eyes glued to our squadron. Of course, it is audacious that our young nation should presume to send its warships to this far-off ocean to fight the corsairs. But I'm afraid that our visit is like a puff of wind as compared with the gales of war that have swept these lands since time began.

"I've a notion these people will take our little visit in stride," he went on. "They and their ancestors have been pirating for thousands of years and I doubt if our squadron can call more than a temporary halt to that nasty business. Even if we succeed, they'll be back at their trade almost before we've sailed for home. One must take a good hard look at their background to understand why that's so."

The blond quartermaster rested his elbows on the bulwark and gazed toward the distant shoreline. "Mediterranean is one name for it, but they might better call it the Sea of Blood. Heaven only knows how many men and women have perished along its shores or lie beneath its surface. No one corner of the earth has had such a prime seat for viewing war. Bloody wars, with whole nations wiped out. In fact, the wonder is that there's anyone left in this part of the world at all, the way these people cut each other down."

Jaime fell silent, his eyes lost upon the North African shore and the mountains beyond.

"You know," he said dreamily, "one reason I signed into the Navy was the chance it offered to see these lands first hand. Oh, I'd read about 'em while I was attending school in Virginia and in England, but there's a big difference between reading about something and actually seeing it for yourself. You'll come to realize also, Andy, that just because something is in print doesn't make it so. The printed word has a power all its own, but keep in mind that it's worth checking and then checking again. Remember that whatever is written stems from a human being. It's reported as seen through someone else's eyes, or maybe something he's heard. And no two pair of eyes are exactly alike."

The quartermaster chuckled. "Sorry I got off the bearing but, as you may have guessed, that's a pet habit of mine, doubting the printed word until I can check it for myself. So that was one reason why I joined this cruise. Not that I didn't want to help stamp out the pirates, but I'm not going to be disappointed if I can pick up the lay of the land while we're in this part of the world. Someday I hope to teach history. If I can make these scenes and these people come alive for my students, why, I'll be well repaid."

The conversation was suddenly interrupted as Sam Plummer came bounding toward them. "Andy, Jaime! Have you heard the latest?"

"Whoa, Sam," smiled Jaime. "If you slow down, maybe we'll find out what's in the wind to get you so fired up."

"A jumping contest! Right here on board," chortled the excited mess boy. "And I've entered."

Jaime's eyes widened and then he began to laugh. "A jumping contest on board a U.S. man-o-war! Now I've heard everything."

"What's wrong with it?" demanded Sam in an aggrieved tone. "It sounds fine to me and, best of all, they've put up a fresh apple pie as first prize. Or a pouch of tobacco if the winner prefers."

"How did they ever get Captain Decatur to agree to such a contest?" asked Andy.

"Agree to it!" snapped the freckled-faced youth. "Why, it was almost his idea. Some of us were jumping over a cask back on the fantail when one of the officers spotted us and suggested the contest. When he asked permission, Captain Decatur said it was a fine idea, that it might work out some of the kinks after the ship's bout with the fever and give everyone something different to talk about. Billy Blossom volunteered to bake an apple pie for the winner and the supply officer said he'd give the tobacco. Are you game, Andy?"

"Sure thing, Sam," Andy answered, though inwardly he feared he'd make a sad spectacle of himself.

"How about you, Jaime?" Sam inquired. "Will you give it a try?"

The quartermaster grinned. "Thanks for the invitation, Sam, but I still feel a mite weak. About the only jump I'm up to is the one to my hammock, so I'll have to settle for watching the show."

That afternoon all hands off duty assembled on the fantail to watch or to take part in the contest. Husky tars were perched on the rail or lounged on the deck. A few had crawled up into the rigging for a better view of the proceedings. Little Billy Blossom was there, blinking in the unaccustomed sunlight, to see how his two mess boys would fare, as were Gunner Ransom and Jaime Rand. About a dozen hands had entered the contest and they were the objects of much mirthful comment from their fellow shipmates.

The after section of the main deck had been cleared as much as possible and, for a starter, four casks had been placed in a row. One by one, the contestants took a short run, each succeeding in making this first jump without difficulty.

Just before Andy took his turn, Bos'n Criter, who was also an entrant, said, out of the side of his mouth, "The Mouse is better suited for crawling into a hole, but don't anybody pop a gun or he's apt to fly right over the mainmast."

The laughter that greeted this sally doubled a second later when Gunner Ransom said dryly, "Maybe so, but if the lad wins, at least he'd be able to down the apple pie without getting sick."

Criter flushed a bright red as he shot the gunner a black look, but he kept his silence after that. Now a second row of casks was placed atop the first as the contest continued. The *Enterprise* rolled and pitched as usual and this time a number of the less spry tars failed to make the jump. When it was Andy's turn again, he gritted his teeth, gave a hard run and flew toward the casks. Just before he jumped, the deck inclined slightly, he barked his shins painfully and tumbled to the deck in a crestfallen heap, amid the jeers of Criter and his friends.

Only four hands survived this second round and, on the next turn, with still more casks facing them, only two contestants remained, Bos'n Criter and Sam Plummer. Andy was amazed that his chunky friend had done so well, but Sam seemed to have springs in his legs. Now, under Lieutenant Higgins' direction, another row of casks was placed atop the three rows already in place. The wind was freshening, filling the sails of the *Enterprise*, and there was now a noticeable increase in the vessel's pitch. Eying the obstacle that now loomed like a small mountain, Andy made a fervent wish that his friend would be able to surmount it.

Even though this was nothing more than a friendly shipboard contest, an air of tension crept into the proceedings. Bos'n Criter, who was to make the first jump, stared soberly at the rows of casks, studying how to adjust his run to the pitch of the ship. As the *Enterprise* headed downhill, Criter was off like a flash. Then, just before he reached his takeoff point, the vessel began its upward sweep. Fighting a losing battle with the laws of balance, the boatswain found himself going uphill just as he left the deck. For a second, it appeared as though he would still clear the hurdle, then his toe caught the edge of a cask. He seemed to waver in the air, then toppled to the deck with a mighty crash, surrounded by rolling casks. A sudden roar of laughter exploded from the audience as the stunned boatswain slowly pulled himself to his feet.

When the casks had been assembled once more, Andy felt sorry for Sam. If the long-legged boatswain had failed, there seemed little likelihood that Sam could succeed either. He held his breath as the chunky mess boy began his run. Unlike Criter, Sam started against the pitch of the ship but, as he ran, the bow of the *Enterprise* began to fall away, giving him added impetus for his takeoff. Andy watched in astonishment as the lad soared through the air, up and up. He saw Sam's feet barely clear the obstacle, then the boy landed safely on deck. He had won!

CHAPTER XII

SAM AND Andy were basking on the fantail in the warm Mediterranean sunshine, taking advantage of a breather in their watch and galley duties, and talking of the recent jumping contest.

"To be honest, Sam," admitted Andy, "I never thought you could do it. Those casks looked high as the moon, but you surely showed your heels to the others. You went so high I thought you might just keep on going." He gave a contented sigh. "And that apple pie was wonderful — the best Blossom has ever baked. It was nice of you to share your prize with me when you might have eaten it all yourself."

"Stow that gab, matey," grinned Sam, mimicking the boatswain. "I had to hold up the honor of the galley and I had plenty of luck to boot. As for the pie, it's share and share alike."

A cry from the forward crow's nest brought an abrupt halt to the conversation.

"Sail ho!" sang out the lookout. "Sail on the starboard beam."

The two boys were on their feet instantly, racing madly toward their battle stations. The *Enterprise* had sighted a number of merchant vessels recently and Gunner Ransom had predicted that the increased number of fat targets would lead the corsairs to adopt a bolder course of action than they had recently been pursuing. There was little question the lookout had spied a pirate craft. If Andy had any doubts, they were dispelled quickly. Crouched low in his position as loader on Gunner Ransom's battery, he stole a glance over the side as the *Enterprise* heeled heavily to starboard.

One glimpse of the black-hulled corsair cruiser, its white sails sparkling against the blue sea, was enough to convince him that this was no mirage. And the pirate craft was heading directly toward them. Judging from its speed, the enemy captain must be eager to tackle the American man-o-war that had ventured foolishly so far from its home port.

Andy found that he was sick with fear. It was all too easy to imagine himself a captive of the pirates, being hauled before the Pasha of Tripoli. He knew that one curt order from that infamous individual might mean he would be minus nose, ears, or arms — a slave forevermore. Or hanged, or maybe made to walk the plank immediately.

Desperately, the slender mess boy tried to shut these thoughts from his mind, to put the coming encounter out of his consciousness. Almost as great as his fear of the corsairs was his dread that his shipmates would discover his cowardice. Then, before he was ready for it, a strange sound assailed his ears, a whistling noise overhead. There was suddenly a jagged hole in the mainsail, followed by a sharp report. Almost before he could realize it, the *Enterprise* was in action, belching flame as it spewed shot and ball over the silver-blue sea.

The succeeding moments became a blur of grime, smoke, and noise, punctuated by the sharp commands of Gunner Ransom. Sweaty, dirty, and exhausted, Andy was dimly conscious of new holes in the sails, a slash through the rigging, and the occasional thump of metal against wood. Now, through the confusion of sound and acrid smell, he became aware that the *Enterprise* was swinging to port again.

"Get ready for a broadside, lads," shouted the gunner. "Cap'n Decatur is going to put us smack against them."

Judging from the stepped-up tempo of the firing and the sharpness of the cannon blasts, the vessels were running on a parallel course. From the growing number of gaping holes in its sails, Andy knew the *Enterprise* was taking a heavy pounding. His head felt as if it were ready to burst and he closed his eyes for a moment to the sight of battle.

"Glory," muttered a tar at Andy's side. "We're closing in fast. Looks like he's going to ram 'em."

Glancing up, the boy saw the Marine contingent tense forward with their pikes, sabers, and pistols, straining as though they were on the verge of leaping aboard the enemy vessel at any instant. A sudden blast exploded almost in his ear and his fingers clawed the wooden deck as the pirate's grape sizzled. Immediately, the batteries of the American vessel thundered back. Pausing for a rapid reload, the *Enterprise* fired again and again. The shots from the corsair slackened off, then stopped entirely.

In the wild confusion that followed, with American tars leaping, shouting, and pounding each other on the back, Andy thought they must be getting ready to board the enemy for a final assault. But it was all over.

"We've won, laddie," cried the gunner, giving him a hearty slap on the back that nearly sent him reeling. "They've struck colors. We've won, Andy."

Through the final swirls of smoke drifting rapidly away, the mess boy saw Old Glory, with its fifteen stripes and stars, flying proudly above the *Enterprise*, and his heart skipped a beat. Captain Decatur had brought them through. The good old *Enterprise* had whipped the corsair.

Gradually, he became aware of the scene on the quarterdeck. Captain Stephen Decatur, clad in his dress-blue uniform, was chatting easily with the officer of the deck as they prepared to receive prisoners on board. From where he stood, it looked to Andy as though the young captain was merely getting ready to hold ship's inspection, so casually did he appear to treat the event. Now, as Decatur rested one leg on the rail, Andy spied the pistol jammed in his boot and a second one tucked in his belt. Captain Decatur was ready for any eventuality.

Burning with curiosity, Andy watched as the prisoners were escorted on board under the watchful eyes of heavily armed marines and tars. Some corsairs were hobbling, others appeared able-bodied, still others were being carried on board by their companions. The boy gave an involuntary shudder as he eyed the unkempt, bearded Tripolitans who had been firing at them only moments earlier. It was easy to visualize one of them running a sword through him. It was almost too easy to imagine the fate of the *Enterprise* crew had the corsairs been victorious.

A sharp command made him jump. Then he saw the wounded marine lying on the deck, the dark splotch reddening through his shirt. What was it the deck lieutenant was saying — something about lending a hand? The command barked a second time. Andy's feet moved forward woodenly as he realized that he had been ordered to help carry the wounded man below. Dazedly, he took another step, then saw the expression of pain on the marine's face. He stooped, then crumpled to the deck.

Much later, sitting in the galley with Sam and Billy Blossom,

Andy flushed with shame as he recalled being revived by Gunner Ransom. Most of all he remembered the grating laughter of Bos'n Criter. But his companions were absorbed in recounting the events of the day and they seemed to have completely forgotten his cowardice.

Listening, the mess boy began to realize a truism of battle. It was one thing to read a newspaper account of a naval engagement, quite another to actually be in one. Reading about it, you had a picture of the entire battle, just as though you were sitting on the quarterdeck with a grand, sweeping view of the action, the maneuvers of the ships, and individual combatants as they grappled with the enemy. Taking part in an engagement was a different matter entirely. You saw only the events that occurred at your battle station, saw only minute happenings that swam within your limited vision as you went about your duties. Sam, stationed aft, had had a fairly good view of the proceedings. Below, Billy Blossom, armed with his cleaver, had seen only his bobbing pots and pans. Andy, stationed at the starboard battery, had actually seen little more than the cook.

The enemy cruiser had been battered badly. Its sails were in shreds and two of its masts had snapped like toothpicks. Grapeshot from the *Enterprise* had cut down many Tripolitans. Some said the ship had lost twenty-five men, including the captain, while others estimated that more than thirty pirates had been killed. In addition, more than fifteen of the enemy had been wounded. The *Enterprise* had not come through unscathed. Besides the damage topside, the ship had lost four men, with nine wounded, two so seriously they were not expected to live the night.

The next morning, Andy stood at attention with the rest of the crew as Captain Decatur, Bible in hand, committed the dead to the mercy of God. Five sailcloth shrouds slipped almost soundlessly into the sea. Five shipmates would never see Boston again.

Winds were slight and days passed slowly as the *Enterprise* towed the captured Tripolitan cruiser toward the port of Algiers. In the general excitement of victory, the tars who had witnessed Andy's fainting promptly forgot about it, but unhappily for the mess boy, Bos'n Criter did not.

Starting to climb a ladder one day, just as Andy moved down cautiously with some hot tea for the officers of the watch, the husky boatswain stopped and gave an elaborate, mocking bow.

"Clear the decks, men," he clucked. "Hot tea coming. Don't startle the Mouse or he's apt to spill it. Then we'd have to splash him awake again."

There was a hearty guffaw from the deckhands who always welcomed an opportunity to stop their holystoning. But Gunner Ransom, working on a cannon nearby, spoke up promptly. "Take it easy on the lad, Boats. Remember, he was loading cannon hot and heavy while you were waving a cutlass in the air and talking about all you were going to do to the corsairs if we boarded them."

"Steer your own course, Guns," Criter retorted, "and let the lad steer his. I reckon he's big enough to stand on his own feet without fainting on your shoulder."

The bull-necked boatswain took a threatening step toward the gunner, then hesitated as Ransom planted his feet solidly on the planking. Only his black stub of pipe moved as he spoke, softly but so distinctly that his voice carried clearly across the deck. "You could be a good man, Boats. If only your brain and hands worked a tenth as well as your tongue, you'd make a deep-water sailor."

One of the seamen grinned and another muffled a laugh. Criter silenced them both with a glare, then started toward his adversary.

"Land ahoy!" The piercing cry of the lookout in the forward crow's nest broke the tension. It also brought a sharp sigh of relief from Andy, still standing on the ladder with his rapidly cooling tea.

"Land ahoy! Algiers dead ahead," came the cry a second time.

"We'll settle this another time," growled the boatswain, turning away.

Excitement rippled through the crew as they made ready to bring their prize into port. It grew as they neared the harbor. The war with Tripoli had been underway since the spring of 1801. Now, two years later, little of a victorious nature had occurred to give the Americans cause for elation. Even the citizens of the so-called neutral nations of the Mediterranean were laughing up their sleeves at the futile efforts of the U.S. squadrons to defeat their brother corsairs. Lately, several rulers of these countries had grown increasingly bolder in their dealings with the Americans. Now, capture of the Tripolitan cruiser, one of the few to be taken these last years, was certain to have a sobering effect upon them.

Andy shared the general exultation, which mounted as they eased into the harbor and eyed the colorful throngs lining the docks. The crowd was swelling rapidly and it was difficult for the men and officers of the *Enterprise* to conceal their pride as they listened to the excited chatter of foreign tongues and observed the stares at the battered Tripolitan prize. Even before the first lines were over the side, Andy spotted the American attaché on the wharf, saw the man cup his hands and shout up to Captain Decatur. His message to the quarterdeck was at first faint and incoherent. Then the words came through more distinctly, their meaning all too clear.

"*Philadelphia* — the *Philadelphia's* captured. All hands taken prisoner."

The bombshell news spread swiftly from stem to stern. Smiles of victory disappeared in a pall of gloom that suddenly enveloped the ship. Andy felt as though he had been struck a solid blow in the stomach.

Losing the *Philadelphia* meant more than losing a good friend. The loss would leave Commodore Preble with only one frigate in his small fleet, the *Constitution*. The *New York*, *Boston*, and *John Adams* already were bound for much-needed overhauls in the United States and there was no hope of recalling them. Even worse than the loss of the thirty-six gun *Philadelphia* was the disheartening news that the Tripolitans had captured all hands. Now the Pasha of Tripoli had three hundred American officers and men under his fat thumb — three hundred hostages to be used as a lever against the U.S. squadron!

The mess boy could not dispel the heaviness in his heart when, later, he made his way slowly back to the fantail where Gunner Ransom, Corporal Ames Whitlock, and a knot of others were discussing the astounding change in fortune.

"Aye, that's the word," Ransom said soberly. "I heard Captain Decatur say that the *Philadelphia* spotted an enemy gunboat about five leagues off Tripoli. Captain Bainbridge ordered full sail and they chased the corsair right up into the teeth of the Tripolitan batteries. But when the gunboat got into shallow water, they had to abandon chase."

John Ransom took his pipe from his mouth and sighed. "That's when bad luck overtook them. The *Philadelphia* was working its way back to deep water when she ran aground on a submerged reef. Of course, they'd been taking soundings all the way, but this

Kaliusa Reef, as the Barbarys call it, didn't show up on their charts. They ran up on it 'fore they knew it was there and found themselves hung up solid.

"As far as I can understand from the officers' talk," Ransom went on, "the Danish consul who sent word to our attaché here said the crew tried every trick they knew in the try to get her free. Captain Bainbridge pressed on full canvas, loosed the top-gallant, and ordered all loose gear thrown overboard. Later, he even had them chop down the mainmast, hoping that would free the old girl, but still she wouldn't budge. Meanwhile, the enemy gunboats, seeing what was up, began to move in on her. They worked their way around to where the *Philadelphia* couldn't bring her guns to bear and started taking potshots at her.

"Despite every trick known to seamen and a few that aren't, she was stuck tight on the Kaliusa Reef. With more Tripolitan gunboats sliding up every minute, Captain Bainbridge didn't have much choice. He could just sit there and let his men be cut to ribbons without being able to return the enemy fire, or he could try to scuttle her.

"According to the Danish consul, that's what Captain Bainbridge set out to do. He ordered the carpenters to drill holes in the bilge and sent the gunner down to open the cock and flood the magazine before he sent up the flag of surrender. But it didn't work out. Knowing those reefs like the backs of their hands, and with the help of all those gunboats, the Tripolitans worked her free a few days later and refitted her slick as a whistle. Now we're minus some mighty good men and the *Philadelphia's* heavy guns will be turned against us."

The brawny gunner rubbed a gnarled hand over his chin. "I

sure wish we'd been there to lend a hand. Even with just a dozen guns, we'd made 'em dance."

Despite the halfhearted effort of some of the older hands to take this new turn of events in stride, Andy knew there was no mistaking the seriousness of the situation. Here they were, thousands of miles from home port, and now the greatly weakened American squadron had experienced the outright loss of one of its major ships, plus hundreds of skilled fighting men. Now Commodore Preble would have to gain the initiative with one lone frigate, his flagship *Constitution.*

"Guns," said the mess boy, "we're a young nation but it seems to me that we could afford more warships. We surely need more men-o-war to protect our merchantmen. Yet we're short of ships and men."

There was little humor in the gunner's grim smile. "I know, lad, it seems that way to me too, but that's the way she is. You know, after the Revolution we had four ships, but Congress got rid of them in a hurry. The ship of the line, *America,* she wasn't finished until after the peace had been signed with England, so they up and give her to the King of France in return for the help the French gave us against the British. Then they sold the *Deane,* the *Washington,* and the *Alliance.*

"I dunno," Ransom went on, shaking his head. "I guess maybe they figured we'd never need fighting ships again, but it didn't work out that way. By 1785, we didn't have a single man-o-war. It left the Atlantic wide open when the Algerians made a treaty with Spain in 1795 and the pirates slipped out of the Mediterranean to make the most of it. In one month, the Algerians, working right out of this harbor, captured nearly a dozen merchantmen.

"Seeing what was up, the other Barbary States wanted their

share of the pie. Finally, Congress got around to ordering some ships and had the good sense to let Joshua Humphrey build them. Since then, we've bought off Algeria and Morocco, but with Tripoli giving us as good as we send, the pirates may —"

The rest of the gunner's sentence was cut short as the messenger of the watch trotted up to the group. "Folger, you and Sam Plummer are wanted on the quarterdeck, right now." Wondering what was up, Andy hurried after the messenger.

CHAPTER XIII

THE OFFICER of the deck with Ensign Harvey, the supply officer, was waiting for them impatiently. "Folger, Plummer, now's the time to lay in some supplies, lads. Fresh fruit, eggs, and, if we're lucky, some goat's milk as well. Billy Blossom has already given us a list of the things he needs. And since you two galley wags work with him, I'm sending you ashore with Mr. Harvey. He has purchase orders which will be handled by the Swedish Consulate. You two lads are to accompany him."

A thrill shot through Andy. He hadn't expected to get ashore and he was only half sure that he wanted to. But Sam's broad grin made it plain that he, at least, relished the opportunity.

"Look sharp, lads," said Ensign Harvey, clapping Andy on the shoulder. "Here's our guide now, courtesy of the Consulate."

Andy stared at the swarthy native who was to show them the way to the Swedish Consulate. The man was small, not much larger than Andy, clad in what appeared to be a dirty white sack, well-worn sandals peeking out from under the folds. He had a nervous tic that caused him to jerk his head sideways. The native seemed less than dangerous, but Andy felt ill at ease in his company.

Andy was pleased to be going ashore all right, but shrank from the idea of being in a strange city in a foreign land. He wondered what the folks back at Boston would say if they could see him now. He saluted smartly and followed the others down the gangplank with mixed emotions. Suddenly his legs buckled and Sam gave a loud guffaw.

"What's the matter, Andy? The feel of land too much for you?" Sam asked.

Andy continued to have difficulty walking. The dock seemed to be spinning beneath his feet, turning everything topsy-turvy. It was all he could do to keep his balance.

Ensign Harvey chuckled sympathetically. "Plummer and I are having our troubles, too, Folger. It's because we've spent so much time at sea that it takes awhile to get our land legs again. Remember how long it took to get your sea legs. This is the same thing in reverse."

Glancing at Sam, Andy saw that what the officer had said was true, for his friend was wobbling up the wharf. Walking on land produced a queer sensation and the thought that he might tumble over made Andy feel slightly ridiculous. But gradually his sense of balance returned. They walked on down the dock which was patrolled by marine sentries from the *Enterprise*. Then Andy felt as though he were stepping into another world.

From the blue waters of the cup-shaped bay, the city had appeared to rise as a white glare against the tawny hills, topped by slim minarets, blue domes, and heavy battlements. Now that distant view was transformed into a kaleidoscope of color close at hand. The area just off the wharf was swarming with natives of every description — Moors, wild-looking Berbers, holy men, and beggars mingled with camels, donkeys, and dogs.

Andy was astonished at the native dress. Long flowing Moorish robes of soft muslin seemed to be the most popular and they were in every color of the rainbow. The more prosperous-looking wore bright turbans or tasseled fezzes.

Andy noted, however, that the great majority of people were clad in rags. He had never seen anything like this scene. And all about him was the smell or, rather, a mingling of smells — from men, animals, fruits, spices, and other strange things that flowed together in a stench that was sickening.

Ensign Harvey grinned at him. "A bit different from Boston, isn't it? Well, don't worry, Folger. You'll get used to it as we put into other ports. After a time, you may even come to miss this smell, though it has quite an impact on one's first trip ashore."

The mess boy doubted that he would ever come to miss the odors that continued to assail his nostrils as they moved into the city. The narrow streets were bulging with humanity and the shimmering heat waves made the odors more pungent.

Crowds clustered thickly about the shopping carts in the bazaar and Andy was hard put to keep up with Ensign Harvey and the others. As he dodged a beggar who tried to clutch his hand, the guide suddenly stepped aside and Mr. Harvey was yanked in the opposite direction. The boy halted in disbelief. It had happened so swiftly he couldn't believe his eyes. A husky native had tossed a burnoose over the young ensign. Another — or was it two others? — had whisked him into a shopping stall. Then they had vanished. Andy stood rooted to the spot. He jumped as Sam gave a startled bellow.

"Whoa, Nellie, they've kidnapped Mr. Harvey! Come on, Andy!"

The two youths plunged through the throng and raced toward the spot where the supply officer and his captors had disappeared. There they stopped, perplexed.

Andy whirled around. "Quick, Sam. There he goes," he cried.

They gave chase, mounting a flight of low steps, when Sam cried out sharply and crumpled to the pavement, gripping his ankle and writhing in pain. "Same one I twisted in the jumping contest," he said through gritted teeth. "Go on, Andy. Try to find where they've taken him."

Andy's decision was as swift as Sam's mishap. "Somebody must take word back to the ship. Can you make it, Sam?"

"Sure can," winced the boy. "You go easy, Andy, and don't get yourself skewered. Remember, all these streets slope down to the bay."

Andy gave a quick wave to Sam, then darted off in the direction the kidnappers had taken. For a minute it seemed he had lost his quarry. But again he spotted them. He crept along the walls, ducking into crevices whenever it seemed he might be spotted, taking advantage of every shadow. Suddenly the kidnappers and their victim slipped through the door of a shop.

Andy was in a quandary. Sweat rolled down his face. What to do? He forced himself to tiptoe forward a few feet until he could make out the sign above the shop. He couldn't understand the inscription but there was no mistaking the picture of an outlandish Moorish pipe.

It was time to seek help. The boy choked down an urge to bolt the scene and to fly to safety. He wondered if he could ever find his way back again. The streets and the shops all looked alike. Then his eye caught something on the pavement. It was Ensign Harvey's epaulet, which must have been torn free. Andy stooped to retrieve it, then, struck with a sudden inspiration, kicked it against the wall.

He reversed his course, halting deliberately at the corner to take his bearings. Now he spied a shop with three gold balls hanging over its entrance, a sign that spelled "pawnbroker" in any language. Slowly, he began to retrace his steps in what he believed was the direction of the waterfront, remembering that Sam had said that the streets sloped down to the wharf. He halted again at another corner. Here there was a small public square. There were more corners and more signs. Andy remembered how his father had taught him to find his way through the woods when he was only a tad and now he called upon those early lessons.

The mess boy was the object of curiosity to the crowd. It wasn't often people saw a young American lad wandering alone through their streets. Andy paid little attention — he could think of nothing but getting to the ship. His feet fairly flew when suddenly he realized he had reached a main street. There he collided squarely with an American naval officer. The impact sent him sprawling. When he looked up, he realized with horror that he had slammed into Captain Decatur himself, who was now eying him with a cold frown. But Andy's dismay quickly vanished.

"Ensign Harvey, sir," he gasped. "They've kidnapped him, Captain!"

"Thieves and thunderation! When did this happen, lad? Where did they take him?"

"Just a little bit ago, sir. He and Sam Plummer — he's the other mess boy — we were with Mr. Harvey on the way to the Swedish Consulate when they threw a blanket over him and toted him off."

Decatur turned to his marine aide. "No time to go to the ship," he said grimly. "Let's see if we can locate Mr. Harvey before they harm him. Do you have any notion where he is now, boy?"

"Yes, sir," replied Andy. "I think I know." Andy began retracing his steps, far more confident now that the captain and his aide were with him. He worked his way back to the square, then found the pawnbroker's shop with the three gold balls. He was sure of the way now.

"There's Mr. Harvey's epaulet, sir." He pointed excitedly. "And there's the tobacco shop where they took him!"

"Careful now." Captain Decatur laid a firm hand on Andy's shoulder. "I hope you've got it right, lad. I don't know how many are in there, but we must take them by surprise if we are to succeed. It's hard to say what we'll find, but I suggest we give it a try. Lad, you keep a sharp eye for Mr. Harvey while we test the brigands."

The two men sidled close against the wall till they were almost abreast of the tobacco shop. Captain Decatur had unsheathed his saber while his marine aide expertly affixed a bayonet to his musket. Andy held his breath.

"Now, lads!" cried the captain, lunging against the flimsy shop door.

Inside, a very fat man, sitting cross-legged on a pile of rugs, screeched in alarm. He tried to rise, evidently with the idea of bolting through a door to a rear room, but the marine's well-placed foot tripped him up and sent him tumbling. Three men were in the rear room as the Americans burst in. They were playing at some kind of dice game. They sprang to their feet, drawing their weapons in one motion.

Andy spied Ensign Harvey instantly. The supply officer was bound hand and foot, a dirty gag stuffed in his mouth. At that moment, Andy was thankful that mess boys as well as deckhands carried knives. He whipped out his knife and slipped past the others, Ensign Harvey watching. The action behind him was fast and furious, judging by the clash of steel upon steel, but he was too busy to look around. He heard a cry of pain, followed quickly by another, but he dared not turn about.

His blade was sharp and served its purpose well, slicing through the cords that bound Mr. Harvey. It was the work of seconds to free him. The supply officer quickly whipped the gag from his mouth. Startled by the sudden silence behind them, Andy whirled. The marine was grinning, even though blood was dripping from a slash on his arm. Using his musket as a club, he had disposed of two of the brigands. The third man had fled after a brief encounter with the captain's steel.

Captain Decatur's dress-blue jacket had been ripped by a knife, but he paid it no heed. "All right, Harvey?" he was saying. "Here, lad, give him a hand. And let's put on full sail before the other ruffian comes back with some friends. I don't know how many more we can handle."

The quartet from the *Enterprise* proved a strange sight for the citizens of the city. Some showed open hostility, but the majority simply stared in amazement. Now that they were back on the main street, Andy saw that Captain Decatur was also staring at him.

"What's that under your arm, lad?" he asked.

Andy looked down and was surprised to find that he was carrying Mr. Harvey's packet. He didn't even remember picking it up in the scuffle.

"The supply orders, Captain," he stammered.

Decatur's gray eyes looked at him keenly. "What's your name, lad?"

"Andrew Folger, sir."

"Well done, Folger. And not just for bringing back the orders."

As they reached the ship a cry of delight went up from Sam Plummer as he spotted them. He started toward them, ankle forgotten, then almost collapsed with the pain.

"Am I fired-glad to see you, Andy!" he exclaimed.

Captain Decatur frowned at this lack of military formality, but Andy caught the glimmer of a smile at the corners of his mouth.

"You two lads skip to the galley and tell Billy Blossom to give you each a fat slab of that apple pie he baked for me. I think you two shipmates have earned it."

The sight of the ship and its flag gave Andy a strange feeling, one he couldn't quite define. Suddenly he realized this was the first time he'd been away from the ship since they had left Boston. The *Enterprise* was truly his home and it was good to have Sam at his side again. What was it the captain had said? Shipmates. He looked up at Old Glory flying lightly on the breeze and whispered the word to himself. "Shipmates."

CHAPTER XIV

A WEEK LATER, with the *Enterprise* still secured alongside the quay, the tempo of living had slowed considerably. There was always work to do on board, but supplies had been loaded and many repairs accomplished. Ropes, sails, and guns had come in for critical scrutiny from the first lieutenant, the gunnery officer, and the men under their command. The decks had been holystoned until the planking looked clean enough for Blossom to serve vittles on it. Andy's knees ached from the hours he had spent scrubbing the deck, which he did whenever he was free from watch and duties in the galley.

There was no way of knowing exactly when the *Enterprise* would be ordered to sea again and it was best to be prepared for a lengthy cruise. But it was plain to Andy that the time in port had provided a much-needed change of pace for the crew. The tars looked rested and fit, thanks to this respite from the sea. And Sam, who had been taking it fairly easy while his ankle healed, began to look positively pudgy.

Andy was lost in reverie as he returned from the dock one evening with an empty slop bucket. Garbage was tossed overboard when the ship was at sea, but in port it was carried to the dock rather than dumped into the crowded harbor. The boy felt a strange sensation as he turned to stare at the city, and there was a lump in his throat. By now the sight of the towers and minarets had become almost familiar to him. At times he even failed to notice the sharp, pungent odors that drifted from shore to ship. Yet, on this particular evening, as darkness fell, this curious city in a distant land seemed even more alien than on the day the *Enterprise* had arrived.

"Stop mooning and shake a leg or I'll have your ear, Mouse!"

The admonition ended in a burst of laughter. Startled, Andy glanced up and saw that he had been almost taken in by Sam's imitation of Bos'n Criter.

"It wasn't proper," grinned Sam as Andy came aboard, "but you looked so doleful coming up the gangway. What are you so all-fired blue about, Andy?"

"Nothing much," replied the mess boy slowly. "I guess — well, I guess because it's Christmas Eve, that's why. This will be my first Christmas away from home."

Sam's voice softened as he threw an arm around his chum's shoulder.

" 'Course it is. I should have known. But you'll get more used to that as time goes by. Men who put to sea are wherever the wind takes them — whether it's Christmas or not. At least we're in a port, snug against a dock, and not hauling sail in a wet gale with black water under us. That's something, Andy."

Sam meant well but his words did little to dispel the loneliness that enveloped Andy as he trudged off to the galley. Billy Blossom shot him a quizzical glance, then nodded his head. "Best remedy for bile or loneliness is work, lad. Here, give a look to these pans. See if you can put enough shine on them to see your homely phiz."

But even Cook's sympathetic growl was not enough to dispel Andy's gloom. He did as he was ordered, but his homesick thoughts continued. It was easy for him to imagine the scene back at Boston — the ring of skates on ice, the lights and merry laughter, carolers shuffling through the snow. He could almost hear the well-loved Christmas carols. Suddenly Andy stared at the cook in disbelief. "Blossom, I'm hearing things. Like singing."

"Are you now?" asked the cook. "Why don't you wander back to a quiet spot on the fantail and clear your ears!"

Leaving the galley door wide open, Andy all but tiptoed back to the ship's stern. The sound of singing seemed to grow stronger — then the mess boy's eyes opened wide. Almost half the ship's company was gathered on the stern. Some lounged on the deck, others perched on the rail, one or two men were aloft in the rigging. One of the deckhands was playing a battered squeeze box, another strummed a guitar, and a third man followed them with his harmonica. The melody was *Adeste Fidelis* and Andy could distinguish Gunner Ransom's deep bass voice. Even Bos'n Criter had joined in the singing.

Shyly, Andy sidled toward a spot near Jaime Rand. At first he joined in very softly, but he soon forgot his self-consciousness and his thin young voice rose high above the rest. A wave of relief welled up in Andy. He had a sudden sense of belonging, a deep feeling of kinship with the others. It really didn't matter much where you were, he supposed. Christmas was sharing — and what better sharing than with one's shipmates?

There was a lull between songs and Jaime spoke as they turned to gaze at the lights on the hill above the city. "It's a long way from home, Andy. But what many of us forget is that Christmas began right here in these lands, in this climate, in this very part of the world. You know, we're much closer to Bethlehem here than we would be in Boston. There was no snow on the ground that first Christmas and those shepherds on the hills over there are much the same as they were centuries ago. This is the way it may have looked that first night when there was no room at the Inn."

The carols ended gently, almost of their own volition, with the tars and marines quietly drifting off to their hammocks before the quartermaster doused all lights. As Andy prepared for bed, he thought about what Jaime had said. It was true. The whole of Christianity had begun in these lands. But just before he dropped off to sleep, his imagination pictured carolers and he heard the merry laughter and muffled footfalls in the snow of Boston.

Christmas Day brought excitement of two kinds. One was dinner, a special repast prepared by Billy Blossom, consisting of a tender, succulent meat dish, a type of yams resembling New England sweet potatoes, plum pudding, and exotic bowls of dates, grapes, and nuts. Fruit was readily available in nearly every Mediterranean city, but Andy wondered about the ingredients of the main dish, which had the crew so enthusiastic they called for seconds and thirds.

"Don't tell any of them it isn't turkey," cautioned Billy Blossom. "I made a special deal with some natives over on shore to buy some lambs, kid goats, and a kind of wild pie they find up in the hills. I mixed them all together and I wouldn't be surprised if there isn't a little camel meat in there, too. But what the hands don't know about their Christmas dinner is all to the good. Let them think what they will and we'll call it Tripolitan turkey."

The second surprise was a visit from Commodore Preble himself. Word was passed quickly that the commodore was on his way to the ship and all hands busied themselves in an effort to put the *Enterprise* in spotless condition. Side boys piped him on board as the tall fleet commander strode up the gangplank, alert eyes taking in every detail as he received a crisp salute from the officer of the deck.

Andy stole a glance at the famous Revolutionary War veteran as he stood chatting a moment with Captain Decatur before going below to the captain's cabin. The mess boy remembered what Gunner and Jaime had told him of the commodore — that he was a firm believer in iron discipline and that he had an irascible temper when aroused. Andy didn't doubt it for a moment as he studied the high forehead, piercing eyes, hawklike nose, and long clean-shaven jaw. Here was an officer who would never need utter an order twice, even if he whispered it. Yet, from the scuttlebutt, Andy also knew that Commodore Preble's discipline had welded the United States fleet into a formidable fighting force. No matter how much the tars might grumble about the commodore in his absence, Andy knew that each of the officers and men under his command were ready to follow him directly into the teeth of enemy batteries and sabers. Their loyalty to the stern New Englander was unmistakable.

When Andy drifted back to the fantail with the others, the welcoming ceremonies were over. There was much speculation among the crew, for obviously a conference with Preble was taking place below.

"You can wager it's something big," grunted the gunner. "Commodores don't leave their flagships and visit a rig like ours just to pass the time of day. He came for more than a spot of tea and Billy Blossom's plum pudding."

A marine who had been standing sentry duty near the gangway

added, "I heard the commodore tell Captain Decatur the *Enterprise* was a fine-looking ship. Said it was first-class and that he liked to see a taut ship."

Later, the buzz of talk on the stern subsided as the quartermaster passed the word that the commodore was getting ready to leave the ship. All hands halted ship's work and snapped to attention as the tall fleet commander took leave of the *Enterprise*. The purpose of his mysterious visit was not long in coming. A sharp order from the deck officer rang out almost immediately.

"Bos'n. Pipe all hands to quarters!"

Andy and the others were already at attention as Captain Decatur emerged from his cabin and walked to the quarterdeck. The captain made a striking figure as he stood erect, caught in a shaft of late afternoon sunlight, waiting for absolute silence.

"Men," he began quietly, "you are all aware of the situation regarding the *Philadelphia*."

Decatur paused as a hum went up from the crew. None of them had forgotten the fate of their sister ship. The news that the *Philadelphia* had run aground and had been captured had hit the men of the *Enterprise* like a thunderbolt. Little was known of the officers and crew who had been captured but, considering the tales told about the Pasha of Tripoli, Andy did not envy their fate. It was bad enough whenever a U.S. man-o-war was sunk and sent to the bottom, but to have a warship and crew captured intact was a mortal blow to the Navy's pride.

Captain Decatur repeated himself for emphasis. "You all remember what happened to the *Philadelphia*, despite the best efforts of Captain Bainbridge and his crew. Word has reached Commodore Preble that the enemy is repairing damage and preparing to float her free. The commodore told me today he is determined that the Barbary Pirates will not use our own ship and guns against us. Yet, protected as she is, lying inside the reef and directly under the batteries of the Tripoli fortress, it appears impossible for us to recapture.

"There is only one alternative," he continued slowly, "and that is for us to destroy the *Philadelphia*. The commodore sketched out a plan of operation this afternoon. I'm sure that each of you also remembers the Tripolitan ketch we captured. The commodore has secured the services of a native pilot thoroughly familiar with those waters. A volunteer crew from our fleet is to man the ketch, disguised as Maltese sailors. They are to take her into the harbor of Tripoli under cover of darkness. They will then blow the *Philadelphia* into such small bits that the enemy will be unable to use her even for kindling wood."

The captain paused, and when he continued there was a note of suppressed excitement in his ordinarily calm voice.

"The officers and men of the *Enterprise* have been offered that assignment, and I have accepted for them. Now—I call for volunteers!"

There was a second of silence. Then a joyous whoop went up as the crew surged forward. Andy stood numbly, rooted to the spot. For an instant he hoped this was all a dream and that he was safely back in his New England hills.

His feet felt glued to the deck and he seemed unable to compel his legs to move. Darting a glance up the line, he saw Gunner Ransom and Marine Corporal Ames Whitlock standing calmly with the others. Sam had hobbled forward, Jaime Rand with him. Suddenly Andy recalled the way the *Philadelphia* had looked under full sail, whitecaps scudding by her. He thought of the men and boys who had sailed her, many of them New Englanders like himself. He swallowed hard and took three steps forward.

As the first lieutenant moved along the line, he pointed to a man here, a man there, motioning him to step out. Gunner Ransom, Whitlock, and Criter were among those chosen but Jaime and Sam were passed over.

"We'll need our quartermaster right here on the *Enterprise*," the officer said to Jaime. "We'll be shorthanded as it is. As for you, Plummer, I'm afraid that your gimpy ankle wouldn't stand up to a running battle."

The lieutenant was about to move past Andy when the mess boy shot him a pleading glance. The officer paused.

"You're not required to go, Folger," he said. "We're looking for the oldest, strongest hands available."

"Please, sir." Andy's voice trembled in its eagerness. "I'm stronger than I look, and you may need someone who can scuttle down a narrow passageway quick."

"You may have a point there, Folger. All right, lad. Fall in with the others."

Bos'n Criter grinned broadly as Andy joined them. "Welcome to the party, Mouse," he whispered. "Let's hope there's no bloodshed this time. We may not have time to revive you and would have to leave you to the cutthroats."

Andy's legs nearly buckled under him. There was no way of minimizing the perils that lay ahead. But now there was no turning back. The die was cast.

CHAPTER XV

CAPTAIN DECATUR'S voice, pitched low, carried to the bow of the boat in which Andy rode. "There she is, men. Our new home away from home." A glint of amusement shone in the gray eyes. "You may not believe it from the way she looks, but I've christened her the *Intrepid.*"

The captain had discarded his epaulets, gold braid, and peaked cap for the garb of a Maltese sailor. Andy had noted that he wore two sidearms and that another pistol was jammed in his sash. His saber was sheathed at his side.

Two boats from the *Enterprise* carried some eighteen volunteers, including Gunner Ransom, Bos'n Criter, and the mess boy. Most were armed similarly to the captain, except that some carried pikes and muskets as well. Andy wore his sheath knife. All hands were disguised as Maltese sailors and some looked so villainous that Andy all but shrank from them. A third boat, manned by sailors who would return to the *Enterprise*, was loaded with combustibles and materials for firing them. It also carried the limited provisions necessary for the voyage to Tripoli.

The *Intrepid* was in almost the same condition as when she had been captured—very dirty. Some of her sails and shrouds damaged in the battle had been replaced, but others flapped ragged and loose in the light breeze. Climbing on board the former enemy craft proved to be quite a different thing from swinging up to the *Enterprise*. The decks were grimy from lack of holystoning and swabbing, and the creaky craft presented a picture of age and indifference to cleanliness.

Gunner Ransom gave a short, explosive laugh. "A raggle-taggle ship for a rag-tag crew. But we'll put things shipshape in short order."

Captain Decatur, standing near by, said regretfully, "I'm afraid not, Guns. Much as I'd like to clean her up, it's important to keep the *Intrepid* looking as much like a Tripoli craft as possible. I do want you to put the guns in shape, those that are workable, and we can square away a few things below. But I want you to let topside stay just as bad as she is."

Loading was hard, sweaty work. The breeze from the southeast had freshened considerably, kicking up whitecaps and causing the boats to slam against the ketch as the tars transferred cargo. The kegs of gunpowder were stored in a forward hold, with the fuses and firing caps aft. Andy's shirt was soaked with sweat from toting explosives up the slippery deck and down into the dank hold. The task was completed just before sunset and he joined the others on the stern to wave a final farewell to the men in the longboats who were returning to the *Enterprise*.

Watching them, Andy thought once again of Jaime Rand, Sam, and Billy Blossom on the mother ship. It would have been easy for him to have held back. No one would have questioned. Some strange force, however, had impelled him to volunteer. No doubt about it, he was fearful of the unknown events ahead of him, but as he turned to look at Captain Decatur, Guns, Ames Whitlock, and the other volunteers, Andy was glad to be among them, glad to be one of them. Men climbed the rigging, the anchor creaked painfully as it was hoisted, wind filled the sails slowly, and the *Intrepid* was underway.

Captain Decatur outlined the general plan of procedure next morning at quarters.

"At ease, men," he began. "Many of you look as if you'd spent a rough night, but the voyage shouldn't last too long, with fair winds. Here is the program I have worked out with Commodore Preble. The main force of our crew will dive below and remain down deck whenever a sail approaches. We can't take any chance of being discovered or our little ketch will be served up the same fate as the *Philadelphia*.

"One of our sister ships, the *U.S.S. Siren*, will rendezvous with us some distance from Tripoli, then drop over the horizon while we make our way into the harbor, arriving, hopefully, about dusk. If we're fortunate enough to sail close to the frigate without discovery, an advance party using muffled oars will row to the *Philadelphia* and set the stage for actual boarding. A second boat will carry the kegs of gunpowder and all hands will execute the placement of the kegs with dispatch. The fuses will be fired at a signal from me or, if I am unable to give the order, from Gunner Ransom. We will then return to the *Intrepid* in the same manner. It is possible the *Intrepid* may be fired upon and disabled in the action. In that event, we will row to the *Siren*, which will be lying in wait just outside the harbor to offer us assistance."

The seriousness of the captain's voice belied his jaunty bearing. "No need to tell you," he continued, "that we will be under the heavy guns of the Tripoli fort and those of enemy gunboats, so silence is the word. One solitary sound could destroy our entire plan, so I want total quiet. Whisper if you must. And, in an emergency, remember that *Philadelphia* is the watchword!"

After that, the days passed slowly. To Andy, each day seemed to take a year, although he was kept busy working with the gunner in order to repair and clean the few cannon in operational order. He also performed mess-boy duties. It dawned upon him slowly that life was much the same aboard any ship. It was work and more work, unending work. The life of a deckhand was hardship itself, with a steady stream of shipboard duties, watches day and night, and constant cleaning when not on watch. Andy hated the drudgery, the back-breaking labor, and the downright cruelty of the sea. And yet life aboard held a peculiar fascination for him. He could not now conceive choosing between land and sea when his tour of duty would be up. If it was ever up, he thought.

The winds fell off while they were still a few days off Tripoli, then darkening skies preceded strong winds from the west. Gales sprang up from nowhere and continued unabated, forcing the *Intrepid* back. Andy prayed that the creaky ketch would hold together, then prayed that she would sink and thus relieve him from his dizziness and seasickness. This was one of the few times he had been truly sick since the first day on the *Enterprise*. The main difference was that now he had less breakfast to lose. Supplies and water were running short and the captain made no attempt to conceal his dismay when Andy reported that many of the remaining provisions were decayed.

"Tell Boatswain Criter to ration fresh water to the very limit — not a drop to be wasted. You divide the provisions down to the last crumb, then tell Corporal Whitlock to set a guard over them."

Captain Decatur smiled as Andy looked askance. "No, lad, I have no fear that any of our volunteers will pirate the provisions.

I mean to guard them from the rats. We'll need every scrap of food to keep our strength up and I don't intend to share with the four-legged owners of this scurvy craft."

Water and food were at emergency levels when the gale subsided suddenly and a warm sun broke through the clouds.

"I'm so empty I could float away like a bubble," Ames Whitlock groaned to Andy who had come on deck. "I'd almost trade my musket for a canteen of cool, clear water. But I'll tell you that the sight of the sun almost makes up for the hunger. On to Tripoli!"

Andy stepped back as their Sicilian pilot passed them silently. He watched as the pilot joined Captain Decatur on the quarterdeck. Taller than most Sicilians, the man was polite to all hands but he kept to himself almost completely. He seemed to have the captain's full confidence but, recalling the kidnapping adventure in the native quarter, the mess boy hoped that he would not betray them.

Andy said as much to Gunner Ransom who had now joined them. The gunner's hearty laugh boomed over the deck. "So that's what's troubling you, lad. No need to worry about our pilot delivering us over to the Pasha. Our Sicilian friend has more cause for disliking him than we do. His brother has been his captive for five years. I should have told you before."

Slowly the *Intrepid* made its way over the now smooth, azure-blue waters of the Mediterranean. Two mornings later, the forward lookout gave a cry that made Andy drop his deck swab and run for the rail.

"Tripoli! Tripoli off the port bow!"

The distance was too great to make out details, but even the outline of the fortress looming up before them seemed ominous and forbidding. There was a queasy feeling in the pit of Andy's stomach as he looked. This was the chief port of the Barbary Pirates, the home base of the raiders who swept the seas of unsuspecting merchantmen. This, at last, was the fortress of Tripoli.

"Easy now," sang out Captain Decatur. "Trim all sails. We don't want to arrive until after dark and this frail breeze gives us an excuse to make haste slowly."

A short while later, the captain ordered the crew to break out two sea drogues to slow the ketch even more. Thankful to be busy, Andy threw himself into the work with a vengence, unrolling the heavy canvas scoops, securing their lines to the stern, then lowering them into the water where they would serve as drags. Now the ship seemed almost becalmed. There was a tense moment in mid-afternoon when a lookout reported a sail making toward them and a closer look revealed that it was a Tripolitan man-o-war.

Gunner Ransom looked worried. "Andy, wake the captain from his nap and tell him that we have a visitor."

Captain Decatur, dozing near the rail, sat up at once and peered through a gun port at the approaching black sail.

"Get the lookout down from the rigging," he ordered. "All hands below, except for the pilot, the man on the wheel, and three deckhands. Tell them to keep their faces away from the enemy if she closes to hailing distance. All men below are to arm themselves and to be at the ready for any emergency."

Orders delivered, the captain resumed his keen scrutiny of the Tripolitan cruiser. Scuttling below hurriedly, Andy was lost in admiration of the captain's calmness in the face of approaching danger. It gave him a large measure of confidence as he crouched on a ladder in the forward hold, poised to spring to the main deck if necessary. He now carried a long black-barreled pistol given to him by Gunner Ransom. The mess boy wasn't sure he would know how to use it but the heft of the gun made him feel better.

Tension grew by the moment, weighting the silence heavily. From his hiding place, Andy saw Captain Decatur saunter across the deck, pick up the swab the mess boy had discarded, and casually put it to use. Finally, a throaty hail from the cruiser indicated the closeness of the enemy and Andy's hands grew clammy. There was an answering hail from the Sicilian pilot. In amazement, Andy watched Captain Decatur lift his swab and wave a greeting to the enemy. In a second, the Tripolitan man-o-war, curiosity aboard apparently satisfied, cut across the bow of the *Intrepid* and continued on her course.

A short time later, Andy responded to a call from Decatur. "Tell the men to relax, lad. It's lucky those fellows didn't spy our sea drogues — but they didn't, and that's what counts. We'll need all the rest we can get."

Dusk was falling as the *Intrepid* edged into the mouth of the harbor. Andy was again below as they neared the city and he found it difficult to breathe as he peeked at the fortress towering high above them. Its heavy battlements and the yawning muzzles of its many cannon left the boy with a smothered feeling.

Sunset came upon them in a swirl of colors as high, feathery clouds drifted overhead. As the big orange-red globe of the sun dipped behind the rim of distant mountains, Andy wondered if he would see it rise tomorrow morning.

Captain Decatur was issuing a steady stream of crisp orders. The drogues were ordered hauled in, lookouts sent aloft, and two tars posted in the bow to warn the pilot of possible shoals or craft as the ketch eased forward. It was dark as the *Intrepid* slid inside the harbor.

"Lucky we've a young moon tonight," whispered Gunner Ransom, "as well as a cloudy sky to go with it — just enough light to see by."

The gunner gripped the mess boy's thin arm, whispering directly in his ear, "Andy, keep an eye peeled for me after you complete your chore. If there's trouble, stand clear and let the older hands handle it. Grab right to my shirttail if need be, because you have friends who want to see you back on the *Enterprise*. I promised Cook I'd bring you back in one piece. If I didn't, Billy Blossom would never forgive me."

The ketch now slipped past an enemy gunboat anchored offshore. Lying flat on the deck behind the rail, Andy could hear the voices of the Tripolitan sailors and, through a chink in the gun port, he could see them playing a game of dice.

Gunner nudged him. "There she lies. So far, so good."

Andy stared hard, then, through the darkness, saw the *Philadelphia*. The *Intrepid* slowly closed the gap between the two ships. They had almost gained the frigate when the wind shifted slightly, blowing the ketch some yards from its prey. Suddenly there was a sharp hail from the *Philadelphia* and the Sicilain pilot answered. Conversation between the two ships continued for some minutes as the *Intrepid* drifted near the frigate.

The gunner's whisper was barely audible in Andy's ear. "He's telling them that we lost our anchor in the gale and is asking permission to make fast for the night."

At a command from the pilot, three of the tars on the *Intrepid* lowered a small boat and rowed leisurely toward the *Philadelphia*. They flung a line to its deck where a Tripolitan sailor caught it and secured it to a bollard. The tars followed with a stern line. The crew of the frigate obviously was still unaware of the presence of the enemy hidden aboard the *Intrepid*. Gunner Ransom now helped another sailor haul in the lines. Captain Decatur and the other volunteers flattened themselves against the deck. Progress was agonizingly slow. At last, when only a brief span of water separated the two vessels, Captain Decatur sprang to his feet. His saber flashed as he cried, "*Philadelphia! Philadelphia!*"

The marines were in motion almost before the command was over. One gave a great leap to the deck of the frigate, landing lightly as a cat, even as the Tripolitans sounded the alarm.

A sentry cried out as a shot from the pistol of the marine caught him full in the shoulder. Others quickly took his place and there was the clash of steel upon steel, punctuated by a roar of sound from musket and pistol. Andy's orders were to stand by on the ketch until the decks were clear of action and then to board the *Philadelphia* with flint and wicks, but now he could not hold back. He leaped aboard.

An almost incredible sight met his eyes. Friend and foe alike were lying on deck. Others raised sabers and pikes. The air was filled with smoke. Blood was everywhere.

Andy shrank back in terror as a Tripolitan with an ax ran toward him. The man swept past, heading for the bowline that held the two vessels together. Bos'n Criter appeared in the darkness. He made a flying tackle that stopped the man in his tracks. The man's fall deflected his ax from its target, but it glanced against the boatswain's leg. Criter fell to the deck. Andy sprang toward him but was caught up short by Captain Decatur himself.

"Quickly, lad. Get those wicks to the gunner. Powder kegs fore and aft, men. Both holds and especially the arsenal!"

Andy caught sight of the gunner disappearing down a forward ladder and scurried after him. Gunner Ransom was breathing heavily when Andy caught up with him, but his hands were steady as he adjusted the fuse.

"It's a shame to make an old man run like this," he wheezed, "but it's great to see this walloping donnybrook. We fooled 'em! The Tripolitans must think we're a hundred strong."

The ship was strangely silent as they raced to the after hatch. The Tripolitan deck force had been put completely out of action, but by now the battle had aroused the entire harbor. Lights began flashing from the other ships and the fortress above them came to life with astonishing rapidity. The cannon of a neighboring ship blasted full away and was followed by a louder roar as the giant guns of the fortress exploded over them.

"Pirates, scum and scurvy!" chortled the gunner. "They couldn't hit the broadside of a frigate if their muzzles were against it. Hand me the fuse, Andy, then skip for it. Head for the ketch, lad. I'll jigger this up and be right at your heels."

Andy could never remember afterwards how he made his way topside and over the rail to the deck of the *Intrepid.* He watched open-mouthed as shot and shell roared over them, splitting the night sky. He saw two marines return to the ketch, carrying a third man between them. The tars returned, singly and in pairs, as Tripolitan grape burst above and about them. With relief, Andy saw Guns come tumbling on board. He made out the figure of Captain Decatur, poised on the frigate rail, whirling a pitch-pine firebrand over his head. The captain would be the last man to return. Suddenly it came to Andy that one familiar face was missing. Bos'n Criter had not come back. Before anyone could stop him, the mess boy made a precarious leap to the deck of the *Philadelphia.* He landed at the captain's side.

"Criter. Bos'n Criter!" Andy said hoarsely.

Captain Decatur's grimy, sweat-streaked face was uncomprehending. "Back, lad. Back to the ketch. She's going sky-high!" he shouted.

"The boatswain, Captain," Andy shouted back. "Bos'n Criter is still aboard."

Captain Decatur pointed to his ear and shook his head wildly. It was obvious that he couldn't hear.

The fire was gaining momentum as Andy spun around and darted forward. Captain Decatur hesitated only briefly, then raced after him. A burst of flame illumined the scene before them as they reached the forward hatch. The Tripolitan with the ax had disappeared, but Criter was half-sitting, his shirt bound around his wounded leg.

Criter gave them a glazed look. "Leave me be, Andy! I'll never make it, Captain. Save yourselves before she blows!"

The burly boatswain might have been talking to the wind as Captain Decatur thrust both his hands under the man's arms and hoisted him to his feet. The three tottered down the deck, Andy supporting Criter on one side, Captain Decatur on the other. The heat was intense. Once the captain's foot slipped and all three were on the verge of going down when the wild figure of Gunner Ransom appeared in the glare from the fire. Wordlessly, the gunner knelt and slung the boatswain over his shoulder as though he were a child. Soon after that, eager hands reached out from the ketch and hauled the party on board the *Intrepid*. Captain Decatur was indeed the last man off the frigate.

Then came the cry, "Bowline cut." There was a similar shout from the stern.

"Away! Away, *Intrepid*," Captain Decatur ordered.

Tripoli Harbor blazed with light and the booming of guns

merged into one mighty roar as the ketch tried to fight its way to freedom. One jagged mast was snapped and the sails were in tatters as the *Intrepid* limped slowly forward.

"We'll never make it, lads," exclaimed the gunner. "We've lost all headway."

Squat and helpless, the *Intrepid* wallowed in the water like a fat duck, the mouth of the harbor still a quarter-mile away. The situation, which had been desperate before, seemed hopeless now.

Andy prayed silently. Suddenly he heard a shout from the bow, then a veritable thunder of cheers. The mess boy rushed to the rail in time to see two longboats glide out of the darkness toward them. The boats were manned by American tars from the *Siren*.

The officer in the bow of the first boat saluted as he hailed the deck. "Captain's compliments, Captain Decatur, and would you all accept a boat ride to the *Siren*?"

There was a moment of disbelief, then an explosion of laughter rocked the ketch as the first man went over the side of the *Intrepid* and into the waiting longboat. The transfer went as smoothly as though it had been a drill and the boats were soon underway. There were two loud thumps behind them as the shore batteries found the range of the *Intrepid* and the craft began listing heavily to port. The longboats had almost gained the harbor mouth when Captain Decatur held up a hand. Andy gaped as he saw that the blazing light from the burning *Philadelphia* had illuminated the entire harbor.

Gunner Ransom broke the silence. "It was a long fuse, Captain."

The rest of his sentence was lost as a mighty blast seemed to lift the longboats out of the water. The sides of the *Philadelphia* appeared to blow up and out, while its superstructure simply disappeared. In the shattering silence that followed, Andy thought that the folks back at Boston must have heard the noise.

The boy saw that Decatur was standing at attention, saluting in the direction of the once-proud frigate. The tars followed suit and saluted without rising from their seats. As Andy slowly brought his hand to his forehead, he caught the captain's whispered words, "Farewell, the *Philadelphia.*"

Captain Decatur sat down heavily. "Row on, lads. Row on."

The brilliant orange-red flames from the vanished frigate had disappeared, but the air still billowed with smoke, hiding enemy ships from view and almost obscuring the fortress itself. It was now safe to return to the *Intrepid.* As Andy turned seaward, the dark hull of the ship loomed above them, furnishing one of the most welcome sights of his young life. The mess boy felt a hand on his shoulder. The captain had been talking to him and Andy hadn't heard a word.

"Folger. Well done, lad. You made the right move back on the *Philadelphia.* We may make a jack tar out of you yet."

Andy saw that Gunner Ransom was at Captain Decatur's side. Beyond him, a pale Boatswain Criter managed a feeble wave of thanks. The captain held up a hand as the volunteers prepared to climb the ladder hanging over the ship's hull.

"Now I'm free to tell you of our next assignment, men. These are the orders issued to me by Commodore Preble before our little shipboard party on the *Philadelphia.* It's back to Boston, lads, for refitting, overhaul, and shore leave. It's high time we scraped a few barnacles. Boston, next port o' call for the *Enterprise.*"

The mess boy sat, almost stunned, as the sailors and marines let out a whoop that must have startled the brigands of Tripoli. Boston! It seemed too good to be true. Boston, worlds apart from the Barbary Coast. Boston — steamed clams, baked beans, and hot apple pie! Old Cony, Mr. Benjamin Day, and his mother. Would they know him? Would his mother think he had changed? What would she think of Sam and Jaime and Billy Blossom?

These and other questions went tumbling haphazardly through the boy's mind. Would he stay in the Navy when his enlistment was up? Would he ship over or would he return to the newspaper business? What was it Cony had said about the lure of the sea?

A hand shook Andy gently.

"Time to climb on board, lad," Captain Decatur said. "It won't do to keep your friends waiting. The *Enterprise* may not have a date with destiny, but she has one with Boston. And so do we."

EPILOGUE

The volunteers who fired the *Philadelphia* in February, 1804, made their escape without a single fatality. Their success added greatly to the Navy's reputation at home and abroad, and added a memorable line to the Marine Hymn. Lord Nelson, then blockading Toulon, called it "the most daring act of the age." The men of the *Philadelphia* fared less well, remaining in confinement for nineteen months. Six of the some three hundred prisoners died before they were eventually ransomed with payment of sixty thousand dollars to the Pasha of Tripoli.

Yet the war with Tripoli was the beginning of the move which ultimately swept the Barbary Pirates from the seas. The American fleet operated under immense difficulty halfway across the world from its home ports, but its feats won added respect for the United States. Commodore Preble succeeded where others had failed. He introduced discipline into the Navy at a time when it was needed most, and yet became the idol of his men. Preble and his officers — such men as Stephen Decatur — inspired ideals of obedience, courage, and efficiency that helped set the high standards of the United States Navy.